There was a flash of movement, faster than any human I'd ever met, and a set of hands grabbed me from the side, lifting me high into the air. With my arms pinned, there wasn't much I could do but kick and scream. I settled for kicking, swinging the back of my boot heel first into the bouncer's ear. He roared with anger and I hoped a lot of pain, but didn't let go.

There was a swirl of movement and the bouncer went still. As if he'd been turned into stone. Not so impossible in my line of work. From what I could see, O'Shea had a rather large knife resting just under the bouncer's jaw. It looked like one of mine that I'd left behind in the root cellar. Good, at least it would be spelled to cut deep and fast.

PRAISE FOR SHANNON MAYER AND THE RYLEE ADAMSON SERIES

"If you love the early Anita Blake novels by Laurel K. Hamilton, you will fall head over heels for the Rylee Adamson Series. Rylee is a complex character with a tough, kick-ass exterior, a sassy temperament, and morals which she never deviates from. She's the ultimate heroine. Mayer's books rank right up there with Kim Harrison's, Patricia Brigg's, and Ilona Andrew's. Get ready for a whole new take on Urban Fantasy and Paranormal Romance and be ready to be glued to the pages!"

— *Just My Opinion Book Blog*

"Rylee is the perfect combination of loyal, intelligent, compassionate, and kick-ass. Many times, the heroines in urban fantasy novels tend to be so tough or snarky that they come off as unlikable. Rylee is a smart-ass for sure, but she isn't insulting. Well, I guess the she gets a little sassy with the bad guys, but then it's just hilarious."

— *Diary of a Bibliophile*

"I could not put it down. Not only that, but I immediately started the next book in the series, *Immune*."

— *Just Talking Books*

"*Priceless* was one of those reads that just starts off running and doesn't give too much time to breathe. . . . I'll just go ahead and add the rest of the books to my TBR list now."

— *Vampire Book Club*

"This book is so great and it blindsided me. I'm always looking for something to tide me over until the next Ilona Andrews or Patricia Briggs book comes out, but no matter how many recommendations I get nothing ever measures up. This was as close as I've gotten and I'm so freakin happy!"

IMMUNE

Books by Shannon Mayer

IMMUNE

A RYLEE ADAMSON NOVEL
BOOK 2

SHANNON
MAYER

TALOS

New York

Talos Press books may be purchased in bulk at special discounts for sales promotion, corporate gifts, fund-raising, or educational purposes. Special editions can also be created to specifications. For details, contact the Special Sales Department, Talos Press, 307 West 36th Street, 11th Floor, New York, NY 10018 or info@skyhorsepublishing.com.

Talos Press® is a registered trademark of Skyhorse Publishing, Inc.®, a Delaware corporation.

Visit our website at www.talospress.com.

10 9 8 7 6 5 4 3 2 1

Library of Congress Cataloging-in-Publication Data is available on file.

Original illustrations by Damon Za www.damonza.com

Print ISBN: 978-1-940456-96-6

Printed in Canada

ACKNOWLEDGEMENTS

Immune was one of those books that came out of no-where and took me along for the ride. As always, my team of editors, I thank Melissa Breau and NL "Jinxie" Gervasio, to whom I owe a great deal when it comes to my books being as clean as they are. Not to mention the fact that I learn something new about writing and edits every time I work with these amazing gals.

This last couple of months have been a bit of a roller-coaster ride, and my family and friends have put up with not seeing me much as I worked hard to bring *Immune* to the table. Thanks for your patience, support and phone calls to make sure I'm still alive.

To my readers, wow, you AMAZE ME! Reviews, messages, emails, and tweets all because you love my characters as much as I do. Thank you, these are the things that make the hard days easy.

My hubby as always deserves a special shout out. He has to put up with a messy house, half-cooked meals, and a wife who mutters under breath about her characters on a regular basis. You are the reason I've come as far as I have. Thank you for encouraging me to push back my fears and chase my dreams; to the moon and back, I will love you always.

1

"**W**ait, what did you say?"

Dox took a slow deep breath, a rattle sounded in the back of his throat that unnerved me even through the phone. It was hard to tell because I couldn't see him, but my instincts told me he'd been roughed up. He hawked a glob of spit, and I cringed. Even for an ogre, I knew there was too much oomph behind it to be just spit. Blood, then, was the only other answer.

"We're in trouble. Louisa is back, and she's blaming you for her disappearance. I'm being pulled in as the one who raped her. Apparently, we want to use her for our own ends, steal her power." Another big breath, and then a cough.

I gripped the edge of the kitchen countertop. "That's not her; she would never do this to us. Dox, what really happened?"

There was a rustle on the other end before he answered, like he was wiping his face with a tissue.

"She had her tribal Guardian pay me a visit. He's coming back in one week to finish the job if I don't admit that it was me who hurt her. Then, he's coming for you. I can't beat him, Rylee. He's too strong."

The old phone creaked under my fingers, a steady ache in my chest reminding me that it hadn't been long since my last battle with seriously badass supernaturals. "Dox, I can't help right now. I'm on my way to a new salvage."

He let out a tired sigh. "Rylee, I've never asked you for help before. I'm asking now."

Dox was one of my few friends, but there was a child out there, hurt and alone, and I was the only one who stood a chance of finding him, hopefully alive. That was what I did. As a Tracker I was the equivalent of a psychic bloodhound able to trace someone's 'threads' no matter how far away, or even if they were alive or dead.

I closed my eyes. Dox could take care of himself; he was an ogre, for God's sake! Besides, there was no way Louisa would follow through on her threat. Sure, the Shaman could be as manipulative as Hannibal Lecter and just as smart; sure, she might try to scare him into doing what she wanted, but I doubted she would really kill him. Louisa was doing what she did best—pulling strings. Dox just had yet to learn this side of her. Still, I felt bad turning him down.

"I've got to go."

I hung up, opened my eyes, and stood there in the kitchen, staring at my reflection in the window. Auburn hair, tri-colored eyes, and a lean body, hardened from years of training and fights, shimmered in the frosted glass. I scrubbed a hand over my face, the slight tremble in my fingers irritating me.

Yup, some friend you are. I gritted my teeth against the thoughts that mocked me. Dox *was* my friend, but this kid I was going after needed me more.

A week. I had to believe Dox could take care of himself. I was needed elsewhere. Maybe if I found the kid quick, I could head down to New Mexico, give him a hand. Yes, that was possible.

I tapped my hand on the table. North Dakota was about to hit full winter mode, and the other states I'd have to drive through to get to Dox weren't far behind on the "Fuck, I'm cold" barometer. The forecast predicted a winter storm for late in the week. If I was to manage my salvage and help Dox, I had to get my ass in gear.

Like now.

I had to meet with the kid's mother in a few short hours at a bar in Bismarck where she worked as a stripper. 'Bottoms Up' was a seedier joint, one I knew of only by reputation. That didn't bother me; it was the kid I was trying to save, not his mother.

"Who was that on the phone, dear?"

Giselle sidled up beside me and I put an arm around her shoulder, surprised by her rational question. "My friend, Dox. He's in trouble." A look over her showed that the little time she'd been back with me and out of her rundown home had done some good. Her color had improved and she'd put on some weight.

On the other hand, her mind was as it had been before. Scattered, with only glimpses of lucidity. Not to mention she'd tried 'running away' multiple times. She didn't like being away from her home in Bismarck, and her spiritual guides residing there.

"Darling mine, won't you help me see the rainbow?" Her light brown eyes were vacant once more. I hugged her against my side, and she shoved me away, eyes suddenly wild with fear.

"NO! I won't let you hurt her!" She bolted from the kitchen and ran out the back door. Grabbing a long winter coat, I followed her out into the frost-kissed air. A sharp, icy blast of wind snatched at my clothes and hair, swirling both out around me, as if it would bare me naked to the wind. Giselle had been my mentor since I was sixteen, had trained me both physically and mentally, helping me hone my abilities. The closest thing to a mother I had, her mind was being eaten by the madness claiming her, slowly stealing her away from the world.

Jogging after Giselle, I ended up finding her at the edge of the barn, cowered against the broken slats and shivering in her thin clothes. Moving slowly, as if she were a cornered animal, I slipped the jacket over her shoulders, clenching my teeth against the frigid air. Son of a bitch, it was bitter already outside; more like the middle of winter than the bare start of it. I couldn't remember the late fall ever being this cold. The air burned my lungs, making it hard to breathe. Giselle flinched when I sucked in a sharp breath, as though I'd hit her.

"Giselle, come back inside," I said, keeping my voice soft. I had to work hard at keeping my teeth from chattering. "It's too cold out here."

The wild look faded and her eyes went blank. I scooped her up into my arms—even with the weight gain she wasn't more than a hundred pounds—and took her back in the house. The wind caught the edge of the door and slammed it behind me, rattling the glass pane insert. Settling her into a kitchen chair, I poured a cup of hot coffee from the pot Milly had started that morning when she'd gotten home from her 'date', and then I grabbed a blanket from my room to replace the jacket around Giselle's shoulders. With some encouraging, my mentor took a sip and her shivering abated after some time, though mine clung to me in tremors.

"There is no child this time," she said, her lips pressed against the edge of the cup.

I squatted beside her, a hand on her knee, feeling the sharp point of bones under her paper-thin skin. "Yes, there is. But my friend is in trouble too. I'm going to try and help them both."

"Always with you, it's the same. Trackers and trouble, they go hand in hand. I remember that much." Her eyes flicked down to mine, lucid. She took my hand in hers and flipped it over to read what was there, to tell me what was coming my way. Despite her talent with reading people and their futures, this was the only way she could 'read' me.

On top of being a Tracker, I was also an Immune. Like a blank slate, psychics couldn't read me, and most spells and magic failed on contact with me. An additional perk was that I was immune to poisons of all kinds. I pulled back from Giselle. "No. I don't want you using up any energy on me."

She snorted and glared at me. "I'll do as I please with the time I'm given." With strength I'd often forgotten she'd possessed when of mind, she took my hand and traced a few lines with the tips of her fingers.

"Choices, many of them will converge. Love and friendship will be tested, loyalties will be divided."

Letting out a sigh she shook her head, wisps of hair floating around her face, giving her a halo when the light hit just right. "Above them all, danger. Death."

It was my turn to snort. "Nothing new about that."

She started to smile, the corners of her lips curling up as her hand squeezed mine, then her lips sagged as the Giselle I knew fled and the vacant stare I'd come to hate slid back onto her face.

Soft footsteps drew my eyes to the hallway. Milly, my best friend and the best damn witch I knew, stepped into the kitchen, watching my interaction with Giselle, wearing a pale pink satin robe and not much else. She could get away with it. Luxurious dark brown hair flowed over her shoulders in gentle waves that looked as though she'd just stepped out of the salon. Where I was lean and tight with muscle, Milly was soft and feminine, her curves giving more than one man whiplash as they passed her on the street.

"How is she?" Green eyes met mine, and I shook my head, rubbing my arms.

"Out of it. Frick, it's cold."

Milly lifted an eyebrow. "It's not that cold out. I came home in my black dress and nothing else and was just fine. Maybe you're coming down with something."

I ignored that comment. The last thing I needed was to get sick.

"Are you going to be around for a while?"

She padded across the hard wood floor to the coffee. Pouring herself a cup she took a sip, then grimaced and poured it down the sink. "You don't mean just for the day, do you?"

"No, I have a salvage, and Dox is in trouble."

She lifted an eyebrow, waiting for me to explain. And in the past, I would have. But in the past, I trusted her completely. Not so much now, even though she was still my friend. Not only had she chosen the Coven over me, which almost cost us both our lives, but she'd claimed the only man I'd ever had feelings for, for herself. Petty of me? Yes, especially since she had no idea that I even liked him, but I wasn't a big enough person to ignore it.

Besides, this last week, something about her had been off. I couldn't pinpoint it, but I'd learned to trust my gut, and something was not right with Milly. For now I'd let it lie, but at some point we would have to talk it out.

The skin around her eyes tightened, but she said nothing about my lack of details. "How long?"

Thinking about what Dox had said, considering the time it took for me to find a kid, I mulled it over. "No more than a week." If it took longer than that I was screwed anyway.

Milly leaned back against the counter, exposing a long line of creamy skin nearly to her navel. Love bites traced their way down and I struggled to hold it together. I couldn't stand the thought of her and the FBI agent who'd been after me for ten years, together. Sure, he knew *now* that I hadn't killed my little sister, and sure, we'd had a few heated moments ourselves, but that didn't mean I had any hold over him. Unfortunately for me, seeing the evidence that they were enjoying each other's company did nothing to ease the building anger. Or the hurt of an unfair betrayal I had no right to.

Seeing my gaze, Milly flushed and shut her robe. "It wasn't here. I went to his house. I didn't break your silly rule."

I'd told Milly when she'd moved in that she wasn't allowed to bring her boyfriends home with her in the hopes I wouldn't have to see her and O'Shea together. It seemed even with the rule in place, I was still going to get to see the evidence. I stood up. "Fine."

"I can keep an eye on her for a few days. I don't have anything urgent to deal with. On one condition."

Shrugging, I nodded. Likely, she wanted me to pick up some ingredient once I got to New Mexico. The state's tagline was "Land of Enchantment"—and that was an understatement when it came to the supernatural. Which was a large part of the reason I'd picked North Dakota; it was one of the quieter spots in the country.

"Sure, what do you want?"

"Take your pets with you. Both of them."

I blinked a couple of times, and then frowned. "How the hell am I supposed to sneak a Harpy into New Mexico exactly? Never mind take her on a salvage." Alex wouldn't be a problem, not really. I'd slip his spelled collar on and people wouldn't see a werewolf, but an oversized dog. But there was no way I'd be able to hide a thousand pound Harpy.

"That isn't my issue. You took them on, and I am not going to be responsible for them when you leave. Giselle is family; they aren't." Her arms crossed, and while she may have been frowning, I could see that she was legitimately upset. I just didn't understand why.

I didn't have time for this. "I can take Alex. I can't take Eve. She's too big. She'll just hang out in the barn."

Milly acted as though I hadn't said anything past 'She's too big.'

"Here, this will hide her; it will make her about the size of a hawk." She held out a coil of bright gold that had been woven into a clasping bracelet. A few diamonds sparkled and danced in the kitchen light. Jaw tight, I snatched it from her. As much as this would be handy, it pissed me off that Milly was giving me grief.

"What's the problem with you? Not getting laid enough?" I snapped as I yanked the crossed shoulder sheath that carried my swords onto my back, then jerked my fleece lined leather jacket over them all.

She ignored my dig. "I didn't ask to take care of them. I did not bring them home. It's enough that I take care of myself and Giselle. If it was my choice, they'd both be sent back to their own kind."

I froze in mid-reach for the doorknob. "Their own kind? You mean the ones who would slaughter them?"

Milly held her ground. "You might be immune to the werewolf, but I'm not, and neither is Giselle. You forget that those around you aren't immune the way you are. Even if he wouldn't act in malice, all it would take is a simple paper cut and a little drool—something Alex is never short on —and I'd be furry for the rest of my life." Milly tossed her hair and continued. "Never mind the fact that a Harpy is hardly safe for anyone to be around. They are not known for their kindness. It's why the black Coven spelled them in the first place, instead of just hiring them."

I shook my head; I was so angry I couldn't even answer her. Both Eve and Alex had nowhere else to go, their 'own kind' didn't want them. Worse, their 'own kind' had put out death warrants on them both. The last of her words sunk in and I lifted my eyes to Milly's. "How do you know how the black Coven was doing things?"

Giselle sat swaying in her seat, the coffee in her hand sloshing over and splashing onto the table.

Milly's eyes flashed. "Don't question me, Rylee. I was kicked out of my Coven over my ties with you."

My jaw dropped. "What the hell are you talking about?" At least she had the grace to flush. "Your precious Coven was trying to kill you; have you forgotten already?"

She strode across the room, helped Giselle to her feet and headed out of the kitchen. Over her shoulder, she cast her final words, green eyes flashing.

"Don't make me take more drastic steps, Rylee. This may be your home, but I will protect myself in whatever manner I see fit. And if that means getting rid of your pets personally, then so be it."

2

"**M**otherfucking whore!" I shouted to the gray, snow filled clouds overhead as I stomped out to the barn. Of all the times for Milly to decide she wasn't comfortable with Alex and Eve, this was not it. Lately, she'd been moody, not sleeping well, not to mention the whole Coven trying to kill her business. No doubt she was on edge, but this was ridiculous. And the timing was oh-so-shitty.

I needed to find this kid, and then book it for New Mexico. I could feel the time ticking down. A week was going to be tight, and I had a bad feeling it wouldn't be enough. At least not enough to deal with whatever the hell was going on. For a brief moment I considered contacting O'Shea. I could use some help with this, but I immediately banished the thought. Let him and Milly go their way, and I'd go mine. A clean break was what I needed if I was going to get over whatever it was I was feeling for the agent. I banged the barn door open, not bothering to be subtle about it, and startled Eve awake. My bad.

A grumpy, thousand pound, half-awake Harpy is not a pleasant sight. The body of a bird, torso, breasts, and head of a woman (albeit large enough not to look out of proportion to the rest of her), she sported a wicked beak from the lower half of her face. Talons gripped the bales of hay she'd been sitting on, crushing them easily. She hissed at me, her beak clacking; her large golden eyes unfocussed as she lunged my way.

"Eve, stop!" I yelled, dropping into a roll and then diving under a swipe of her claws. Using her name should have snapped her out of this, but for some reason, she didn't respond. Dodging and diving between barn posts, I kept her at bay. "Eve, wake up!" I didn't want to hurt her, I was her mentor now, the last thing I should have been doing was sticking her with one of my blades. Besides, I suspected being wounded would only make her more pissy; not the effect I was going for. I pressed up against the back of the barn, the big doors behind me creaking before I finally pulled a sword.

Letting out a screech, the Harpy came at me, beak wide open, her eyes shut. I raised my sword, prepping myself for the blow.

A flurry of black and silver whipped between us.

"Evie, bad!"

Eve froze and blinked twice, then looked down at me and my rescuer. "Alex?"

He frowned up at her, and then struck one claw over the other. "Bad, Evie. No hurt, Rylee."

She looked over at me, then bobbed her head, eyes clearing as she came fully awake. "I'm sorry. I was having a bad dream about a demon and thought I could smell him."

"No shit, you were having a bad dream." I grumbled, sliding my sword back into its sheath. "Alex, you're going to come with me, we've got some work to do and then we're going to see Dox."

Amber eyes lit up as he started to hop and jump around my legs like an excited puppy. "Brownies!" He yelped.

"Yeah. Maybe."

I fingered the gold bracelet in my pocket. I couldn't ask Eve to wear it, not after the spell the black Coven had used to control her consisting of a large ruby buried in her foot. There was still an imprint in her flesh where it had been buried and used to control her. "Eve, you will have to find somewhere else to roost while I'm gone."

Alex frowned up at me. "Evie come?"

"No, Eve can't come. I can't hide a Harpy."

She sat back and preened her feathers. They'd gone from a greasy brown to a glistening sable and tan with a little extra care. "You are my mentor. I should come with you. To help, and to learn."

I held back a groan, teeth clenched. "I can't hide you, Eve. You're too big." I rubbed my hands over my face, the air around me crackling with cold. "Listen, I have to go to New Mexico after my salvage. You could go ahead of me, stay with my friend Dox until I get there. Can you do that?"

She paused in her grooming. "I can fly quickly. I can be there in no time."

Okay, that was one problem dealt with. What I would do with her once I got to New Mexico was beyond me, but at least Milly wouldn't be doing anything drastic. I put a hand over my eyes; the only thing that would make this day worse would be O'Shea showing up to see Milly. I didn't think I was ready yet to watch them play kissy face.

The sound of a vehicle pulling into the yard jerked my head up. I peeked out the barn door to see O'Shea step out of a black SUV. Damn, I just had to think of the worst-case scenario, didn't I?

Dressed as a typical FBI agent, he wore a dark suit under a long black trench coat, sunglasses and with his raven-colored hair slicked back. Man in black and all that jazz. Not so typical in that he was one of a very few people that knew the supernatural existed, I mean, truly 'I believe in dragons' kind of knew.

"Shit."

Alex peeked out the crack in the door below me. "Man with gun."

"Yes, now shush."

I should have been prepping to leave, should have been piling my gear into the Jeep and peeling out of here. But O'Shea was walking up the steps and knocking on the door. A terrible, masochistic side of me wanted to see them together. Only then would it be real, only then could I—maybe—let go of this silly hope he might have more than professional feelings for me. Stupid, I know.

Milly came to the door, still in her robe, which gaped open completely with a gust of wind; even I could see her bare breasts—there was no way he'd miss them at that range.

"Nipples." Alex muttered.

Good grief, no man was safe from her charms.

I couldn't hear what they were saying, but Milly leaned over, pressing herself against O'Shea before pointing to the barn. He glanced over his shoulder and I pulled back from the door.

"Time to go," I said. So there, I'd seen them together. I knew they'd seen each other over the last week. Milly had said it was for coffee, but that was just one of her many code words for sex. It didn't bother me. Nope, not one bit.

Alex bunted his head into my hand, "Rylee sad."

A single deep breath. "Nope. Not sad." I scratched him behind one floppy ear. "We've got to go now. Eve . . ." I turned to see her head nearly on the ground, large blobs of moisture gathered in the corner of her eyes.

A crying Harpy? I did not have time for this! Doing my best to keep my voice even, I asked, "What's wrong, Eve?"

"You do not want me now, I am a burden."

The barn door creaked open and a swirl of cold air and snow whipped in.

"Adamson, we've got a problem."

"Damn, just add it to the pile," I snapped, striding over to Eve, softening my voice. "Listen, I do want you with me, but do you really want to wear this?" I pulled the large bracelet out of my pocket. "It's just like Alex's collar, you wouldn't be seen for what you truly are; in fact, it would actually change you, making you small enough to ride in the Jeep with me."

She recoiled as if I'd slapped her, wings going wide as she scrambled away from me, knocking over bales of hay and generally making a ruckus that could probably be heard back at the house. I waited for her to settle down, my hands on my hips.

"You would spell me!"

Shaking my head, I answered her. "No, that's why I didn't suggest this. It's why I would prefer you would go ahead of me to wait for us. That's it."

Alex sat between us and flopped a wave at O'Shea. "Hi ho. Alex going for car ride." He grinned, tongue lolling out between his teeth.

"Where are you going? Milly wouldn't tell me." O'Shea asked, coming to stand beside me. I could smell him, even over the hay and dust of the barn. His cologne tickled my nose and made me want to bury my face into the crook of his neck. I glanced over and it was as if the cold wind from outside snuck in and whipped up my spine. "You've got lipstick on you."

He grunted, lifted a hand to the small bare patch of skin on his neck, and wiped off the stain but said nothing about it. Fine. I could pretend like I didn't care too.

"You didn't answer my question."

Shifting away from him, I blew out a breath. "Because right now I'm dealing with a rather more pressing issue." I pointed at the Harpy who was all but cowering in the corner. It was so easy to forget that while she was huge and could kill with ease, she was still a child; she still needed the basics: love, attention, care.

"Eve, the only way you can come with me right now is if you wear this." I held the gold bracelet up again and she hissed at me. "If you don't want to come, that's fine. I won't make you do anything you don't want to. You can go ahead on your own to meet me."

I laid the bracelet on the ground. "You remember where I'm going?" She bobbed her head.

"You would let me decide?"

"Yes. Either way is fine. Just leave when I leave."

O'Shea touched my arm, tugging lightly on my leather jacket. "We need to talk."

"We can talk here."

"I don't want an audience." Like a werewolf and a Harpy would have anyone to spill their guts to. Still, I followed him out of the barn, albeit reluctantly. As the door shut behind us, he stepped so close he was in my personal space—as in our bodies were brushing up against one another. In the past, he'd used this trick for intimidation, but it didn't feel like that was the case now. I moved back and he followed until my back was pressed against the wooden boards of the barn.

"Hey, mind giving me some room here?"

"No, we need to talk. You've been avoiding me and Agent Valley. He wants an answer. He needs to know if you will work for him. The AA division could use you; they're floundering trying to play catch up with the supernatural."

I couldn't stop the words, they slipped out before my filter kicked in. "And what do you want?"

The cold, wind, and world seemed to disappear around us. All I could see was his midnight dark eyes, the line of his jaw and lips. He swallowed, his Adam's apple bobbing.

"I want . . ."

Alex took that moment to burst out of the barn, spinning as he chased his tail. Before we could move, he rammed into our legs, knocking us both to the ground. That's what I get for letting myself be distracted.

The ground was frozen, hard, basically unforgiving. And it hurt like hell when my back slammed into it, O'Shea landing on top of me. The air rushed out of me in a whoosh, the weight of O'Shea not helping one bit.

"Off," I managed. O'Shea did a push up over my body and stood, then offered me a hand.

I lay there waiting for my lungs to reconnect with my brain. Finally, I was able to suck in a breath of cold air that burned its way down my throat. Ignoring O'Shea's outstretched hand, I rolled to my knees, then stood.

Alex was already at my Jeep, hopping and jumping in his excitement, claws digging into the paint as he worked at popping the handle open. It was hard for me to get mad at him; he didn't mean any harm. Milly's words came back to me. A part of me knew she was right; it would take a seemingly harmless bite from Alex and Milly would be turning fuzzy, maybe on a permanent basis. The other part of me wanted to smack her upside the head. She was the best goddamn witch around and she was afraid of one silly, submissive werewolf? Something was way off with her; I just had to figure out what. Add it to the list of problems.

"A penny for your thoughts," O'Shea asked, holding out a polished coin to me. "They look dark and brooding. Are you going on a salvage?"

Ah, if only it were as simple as returning a child home. I lied, hating to do so. As much as I had only moments before been considering his help, I knew my mind would only be thinking about him and Milly in bed. Nope, not a good place for the psyche when on a salvage.

"No. Not today."

I walked toward the root cellar. The entranceway was at the back of the house. Flakes of snow drifted down, the first of the year. It was later than usual. Maybe global warming, but more likely some damn weather elemental had its knickers in a knot.

"Adamson."

My shoulders tightened when he used my surname. It was the only thing I had left from my past, from parents who didn't want me and a little sister I was accused of murdering.

"Don't call me that."

His footsteps faltered. I slid the bar back on the old root cellar and flung the doors open. Dug out under the house, the cellar was a cool dry place, perfect to keep weapons and gear clean and ready for use. After trotting down the cement stairs, I breathed in deep. There was still the faint scent of smoke from the black Coven trying to kill me and Alex, but there was also the hint of onions and some other vegetable I couldn't identify from the previous use of the area.

I flicked a switch screwed onto an old piling that held the house up, and light flooded the room. With precise movements, I piled up the things I would need. Swords, blades, rope, flak jacket, first aid, and finally a coiled whip I'd only just added to my list of weapons.

O'Shea ducked his head in and frowned. "You have everything you need?"

The sarcasm in his voice was not lost on me. "Nope, forgot this." I held up a black box that held a bunch of ready-made spells—courtesy of Milly—that was locked tight.

"And that is?"

"None of your business." I brushed past him with my gear, made my way to my Jeep, piled it in, then went back and shut the cellar up. O'Shea hadn't moved an inch.

"Rylee."

My name on his lips stopped me in my tracks. I lifted my eyes to his, tried to figure out what was going on behind those nearly black eyes. What did he really think about me now? Or had his opinion not changed?

"What happened? I thought we'd moved past these games," he said. "I thought you would want to work with me, finding kids, helping them get home."

I couldn't tell him the truth—that I wanted nothing more than to jump him, strip his clothes from his hard body, and taste every inch of him. Which of course had nothing to do with finding kids, not one bit. Never mind; he'd already chosen Milly. No need for me to rub salt in my own wounds. So I told him the other truth, the one that separated us as much, or more than Milly did.

"You do things the right way. By the book. I can't, not in this world." I lifted my hands over my head. "If I did everything by the book I'd be dead by now. If Giselle had gone by the book and put me in foster care, if she hadn't taught me to fight, how to use a blade, how to hone my skills, I'd be dead a hundred

times over. You can't tell me the FBI is going to welcome in a rogue like me. Not truly. And the first time
I fuck up." I snapped my fingers, the meaning clear,
but I said it anyway. "I'm done."

"You don't know that."

"I do. And now I have to go." Spinning on one heel,
I strode to the Jeep, and let Alex in. He clambered up,
all but vibrating with excitement.

"At least tell me what's going on. Let me help you."
I could hear the anger under the words; he was barely
holding it in. He was trying, and I wished to hell I
could take him up on his offer.

Oh, how I wanted to believe him, how I wanted
to think he would be *that* man in my life, someone I
could depend on. But, I couldn't, and I knew it.

Turning my back on him I slid into the Jeep. "It's
none of your concern, O'Shea." And slammed the
door shut.

3

None of his concern? O'Shea watched Rylee pull away, Alex bouncing like mad in the passenger seat. Slipping his sunglasses back on, he made his way around the side of the house and knocked on the front door.

Milly, Rylee's friend, came to the door, opening it up wide. She was still wearing her skimpy robe, her long dark hair dishevelled. It looked as though she'd just stepped off a porn set.

"Well, Mr. Agent man, you came back for what exactly?" Her words all but purred out, dripping with a sexual fever that perhaps in another time, he would have welcomed. As it was, he cleared his throat and kept his eyes on her face.

"Where is she going?"

Milly pouted, reached out and tugged on his tie. "If you come in, maybe I'll tell you. You know, we only ever got to chat that one time, and you were in such a hurry that you ran off before I got to know you at all. It's funny; In all these years, Rylee never mentioned you were such a handsome man. She only ever complained that you were an asshole trying to pin charges on her. I have to say, I was surprised—pleasantly—when we met."

He clenched his jaw, and his anger surged, partly at Milly, partly at Rylee's assessment of him. "Tell me where she's going."

A frail hand appeared from behind Milly, and the door cracked open further to reveal a woman who looked to be in her late eighties by the way she was partially slumped over and the pallor of her skin, but he didn't think that was the case. Brown eyes narrowed, taking him in.

"You are looking for our Rylee?"

Milly snorted, folded her arms across her chest and waved at the older woman. "This is Giselle. Sometimes mad, sometimes lucid. Rescuer of forgotten children."

"Don't sass me, Milly. I can still spank your bottom if you give me grief."

Milly seemed to fight back a smile at the older woman's reprimand, and O'Shea liked her better for it. As far as he'd seen, Rylee was a far better friend to Milly than the other way around, which didn't leave the sultry witch many redeeming qualities in his eyes.

Giselle reached out and took his hand, pulling him into the house. "Come, let me have a look at you."

A shiver slid over him as her fingers grasped his with a strength that surprised him and confirmed she wasn't as old as she looked. Her eyes narrowed and she took in a short sharp breath through her nose that whistled. That wasn't what freaked him out though. It was the sound of voices that began to whisper around him.

"Tell him."

He swallowed hard. The world he'd known was disappearing faster than he was truly comfortable with. "Tell me what?"

Both Giselle and Milly started as if they'd been pinched at the same time. Milly stepped forward, her face devoid of any sexual machinations, and green eyes wide with surprise.

"You heard them?"

Giselle started to chuckle. "Oooo eeee. Rylee picked herself a good one."

O'Shea couldn't move. He had a desire to back out slowly, shut the door, and pretend this encounter hadn't happened.

Milly tucked her robe tight around her body, covering herself finally. Her eyes softened with worry. "Damn. Come on in. I'll tell you what I can."

O'Shea followed her into the kitchen, Giselle chuckled and snickered at a distance, standing in the doorway and peering at them like a child might when a stranger comes for a visit. He didn't sit down, but stood behind a chair. He didn't want Rylee getting too far ahead of him.

"I just need to know where she's going. Until she agrees to be my partner, I have to keep tabs on her."

Milly motioned to the pot of coffee and he nodded to be polite, chaffing at the time delay. He had to play this right to get the information he needed. Pouring him a mug she asked, "How is that different than before?"

He took the drink from her. "I'm looking out for her now."

Giselle sidled in, eyes darting to O'Shea, then to Milly and back again. "Blue socks. Rylee needs them. And you," she pointed at O'Shea. "You both need them."

O'Shea lifted an eyebrow at Milly. She pursed her lips. "Like I said, lucidity comes and goes for her." She took a sip of her coffee, grimaced, and stared at him over the rim, green eyes challenging him. He liked this side of her better; this was the Milly he could see being friends with Rylee.

Letting out a breath, he put his cup untouched on the table. "Tell me where she's going and I'll get out of your hair."

"Her friend Dox is in trouble. But she's got a salvage first. She's heading to a bar in Bismarck to meet with the mother of the kid. 'Bottom's Up,' I think."

His eyebrows rose sharply. That was a strip joint. Not that it mattered, if that was where Rylee was going, he would follow. A sharp nod and he turned to leave, stopped only by a hand; Giselle again. He stared down at her, shocked to see a sharp intelligence in her eyes.

"She needs you. She just doesn't know it yet. There are people who would manipulate and use not only her talents, but her grief, against her."

His lips clamped shut, unable to say anything to that statement.

Giselle tightened her grip on his hand, her eyes suddenly welling with tears. "Rylee will die if she doesn't let you into her life."

Ice trickled down his spine. "Then I'd better get going after her."

The old woman, nodded. "And be warned, Liam. The darkness that seeks her life will seek yours. It doesn't want you at her side and will do anything to keep you apart. It will use any means necessary to turn you two against one another. It will make you fear and hate yourself. You must rise above it all."

How had she known his first name? He wasn't sure he wanted to know what was going on. He'd gotten what he'd come for, gotten more than he'd bargained for. With care, he finally pulled his hand free, and Giselle slumped into the chair; he glanced at Milly. The witch was silently crying, a hand trembling at her lips, though she said nothing.

"You believe this?" He motioned to Giselle who seemed to have passed out, head pillowed on her arms on the table.

Milly wiped at her eyes. "She's never been wrong."

Without another word, he turned and strode out of the house, the ice wind cutting through his clothes as he stepped outside. He grabbed some weapons from the root cellar, mostly blades, as he knew how to manage those.

Driving off the farm, he looked around at the quickly whitening landscape and the white flakes thick and heavy with moisture.

"Of all the days, Rylee." His lips quirked as he said her name. She needed him, even if she couldn't admit it. And that sat just fine with him. Just fine, indeed.

"Alex, get back on your side!"

He did as I asked, though he continued to bounce in his seat, actually rocking the Jeep from side to side. His breath fogged up the windows something fierce.

I cracked my window and said, "Roll down your window, Alex."

"Snow, snow, snow, snow!" He chanted, not bothering to keep his volume down as he scrambled with his window, rolling it halfway down, a blast of cold air filling the Jeep.

Unfortunately, he was bang on. The white stuff had been falling steadily for over three hours and the road crews seemed to be taking the day off. There was a thin goat trail for vehicles where there should have been two full lanes. The other side of the highway didn't look any better. We should have been into Bismarck already, but we were maybe halfway at best. Shit, I was going to miss my appointment.

Windshield wipers on high, the snow was so heavy it was like driving through a swirling fog, and I leaned forward to get a better view. Middle of the day, lights on, and I still couldn't see where the hell I was going. Not a good start to this little trip.

The wind blew hard, throwing the Jeep sideways. Fighting the steering wheel, I cursed under my breath. Immune I might be, unable to be turned into anything furry or bloodsucking, and a Tracker of children using my innate abilities. But, I could still be killed. And driving in bad weather like this was not one of my talents. It was the only downside to living where I did, in my opinion.

"Come on," I grumbled at the weather. Anger was easier to hang onto than fear. Better in this case, 'cause being afraid would only give me more trouble.

"Come on," Alex grumbled, shaking a fist at the windshield. Shit, that werewolf made me laugh. I hated to admit he was one of the best things that had ever wandered into my life.

And what about O'Shea? Well, I didn't think stalking me for ten years counted as 'wandering into my life.'

Besides, he'd been hanging with Milly; they were lovers, while he and I were . . . what the hell were we? Not friends, not enemies, something in between. Fifty shades of gray, my ass; there were at least a thousand, if you asked me.

My heater took that moment to kick off and within moments the cab filled with icy cold air. Alex didn't mind, his thick coat perfectly suited to the weather, but a sharp pang in my chest shot through me. I tried to draw a breath, struggled to get a gulp of the cold air. What was happening? I took my foot off the gas pedal, let the Jeep start to slow down on its own as I fought the now crushing pain in the middle of my chest. Each breath I took rattled in my throat, as if I were sucking in water as well as air. Hands clenching the steering wheel, I tried to pull over, but my muscles wouldn't respond, my foot not even reacting when I made an attempt to lift if off the gas pedal. A flicker of an image danced in front of the Jeep.

The last salvage I'd completed involved a demon. We'd fought and I'd beaten it with a little help from my friends, but it had nailed me with its stinger before dying. The demon's antennae twitched in the wind, its black body standing out in the white snow. Shaped like an ant standing upright with a scorpion tail arcing over its head, I knew the thing could fight, but we'd sent it back to where it'd come from. Hadn't we? Shit, I thought we'd killed it. Maybe not.

The demon faded out from in front of the Jeep and I let out a breath, forcing the air from my lungs. I must have been seeing things, my eyes playing tricks on me. Like an asthma attack, I struggled for each breath, but pushed on driving. If I stopped here, there was a good chance we'd not be found until morning, and if the temperatures dropped, well, let's just say I had no intention of being a Popsicle anytime soon.

Alex started to bark, a high-pitched sharp, fear-filled staccato that burst through the fog of whatever was happening to me.

"Rylee, Rylee, Rylee!"

I opened my eyes, unaware I'd even closed them. Right in front of us was a grader, horn blowing as I drove straight toward it.

I yanked the steering wheel hard to the left. The Jeep slewed around the larger vehicle and into the deep snow on the side of the road.

"Fuck!"

The edge of the road disappeared into whiteness when the Jeep hit something hard, snapping it up, flipping us ass over tea kettle. The world seemed to go still as we floated for a brief moment, and I fought to stay conscious.

We landed hard, but the snow partially cushioned us—the only good thing to happen so far. Groaning, I hung upside down in my seatbelt, the material digging into my chest, increasing the pressure on my sternum, driving me to the brink of blacking out. The cold filled me, but didn't numb me. Cold fire raced through my veins, my body spasmed.

Alex whimpered, licked my hand, but I couldn't stop the tremors. I had no control over my own body. Only my eyes would do as I commanded and that didn't exactly help. The windshield was caved in and I stared at the white snow, again the image of the demon dancing in front of me. Laughing.

"Bastard." I coughed and spit at the snow. Blood flecked the white, my lip split from hitting the steering wheel.

"Alex, go," I said, my voice a bare whisper.

"No, stay with Rylee," He leaned forward to put his face close to mine, balancing on the steering wheel and hitting the horn before settling off to one side. I wanted to cover my ears, but couldn't even lift my hands. Was I paralyzed? Now that would seriously screw up my life.

Dark spots and bright lights swirled in my vision. In desperation I reached out with my abilities to the one person I knew I could hang onto.

Tracking O'Shea was easy, his mind an open book to me. And he was a hell of a lot closer than I'd expected.

He was close enough that his emotions were right inside my head, less than a hundred feet away. Confusion, anger, and worry were at the front of the line and they swamped me with their intensity. Pulling back from him, I tried to lift my hand, to no avail. "Alex. Horn. Hit it."

Alex reared up and jammed both front paws onto the horn, the sound jarring my senses. Nausea rolled over me and vertigo hit me hard, made me want to throw up.

The dark of unconsciousness swallowed me whole between one breath and the next. Distantly, I could feel hands on my body, a voice I knew speaking softly to me. But what I was seeing inside the darkness held my attention.

I'd met this one before, on the other side of the Veil, after we'd rescued India. He stood watching me, an eyebrow quirked up into his hairline. Crystal clear blue eyes regarded me. "You have yet to even ask my name."

I frowned. "I don't care what your name is."

He smiled. "You may call me Faris. Will you speak with me?"

The darkness seemed to shift around us, putting me only a few feet away from him. I tensed, confused by the feeling of hands on me while I could see that he hadn't touched me. "I think I'll pass." The thing was, I couldn't turn away from him; my body still wasn't obeying me.

He tipped his head to one side and stepped closer to me. "The demon that struck you was a Hoarfrost demon. It is designed to turn its carrier into an epicenter for a new ice age. Of course, that only works if the venom can be assimilated. Not the case with you. However, it is slowing you down. Until you deal with it, the cold will follow you, make you vulnerable to all sorts of nasty things." He leaned closer, his breath brushing across my cheek.

Panic clawed at me. "No, I'm an Immune. I can't be killed by venom."

"I didn't say it would kill you, not the venom at least. But it's hurting you nonetheless, and the side effects of it, they could kill you. You aren't immune to hypothermia. It makes you vulnerable, unable to defend yourself. I quite like the change in you." He lifted a hand and brushed it across my cheek, then down to my bottom lip, tugging at it.

I jerked my head away, the only part of me I seemed to have control over. "Why would you tell me this?"

"I want us to be friends."

Laughing, I threw my head back. "That's why you tried to kill me?"

Faris smiled at me, a glimpse of fangs coyly peeking out from beneath thin lips. "You'd upset me. I hadn't expected you to turn from me as you did. Do you know how long it's been since I've had a woman turn me down?"

"Obviously not long enough."

Ghost hands slid over my skin and I shivered recognizing O'Shea's touch. Then those hands that were being so gentle slapped my face, snapping my head to one side.

Faris laughed. "I will tell you one thing because I want you to trust me. There is a way to purge the demon venom. Ask Doran, he will explain. Until then, try to stay warm. Or you could wait for it to run its course, hiding somewhere the snow never flies. That might take a few years." He lifted his hand, fingertips brushing lightly along my jaw line. "Even Immunes can be hurt, Rylee. Remember that."

He gave me a slow smile and I glared at him. Not exactly an effective deterrent.

"Perhaps we will speak another time." He was suddenly holding me tight, his lips above mine, fangs extended. Panic clawed at me; I couldn't fight, couldn't even begin to push him away.

I screamed, pushing all my energy toward shoving him away, and a bright light burst beside us. It was his turn to scream, fleeing from the bright pulsing light as I crumpled to the ground.

Hands caught me, a face I saw only in my dreams hovering over me.

"Berget," I whispered. She smiled down at me, blue eyes sparkling with love and laughter.

"Rylee, be careful. Faris wants you badly, and he will do anything to gain your trust. This one time, though, he is right. Go to Doran."

This was not like the dreams I had with her in them. This was real; she was here with me.

"I can't find you," I said, tears choking me. "I keep trying but . . ."

She shushed me. "I know. I don't blame you. This is no one's fault. This is destiny. You will understand in time." Leaning over me, she kissed me on the forehead and I opened my eyes to see O'Shea leaning over me.

"Adamson!"

I managed a weak, "Hey." Then I promptly closed my eyes. I wasn't out of it, I just couldn't look at his face, see the worry and concern there. I didn't want to feel anything right now. My emotions were a jumble of my own and O'Shea's, and I was struggling to separate them. What had happened when I blacked out? Had I really spoken with Berget? Was she alive somewhere? Was Faris really able to contact me when I was unconscious? That would not be good.

A cold, wet nose jammed into my ear.

"Alex scared."

O'Shea lifted me up like I was nothing, cradling me against his chest. The world tilted as he walked, and I could hear sirens in the distance.

"We have to go," I mumbled. "I'm okay, I just need to warm up."

O'Shea didn't stop moving. "You were in a car accident, you are not okay."

"Not the accident. The demon. From before." Hating that Faris was the one to cue me into my problem, I could now feel the venom pumping through my system. It was slowing everything down, making it hard for me to keep breathing. There had to be a way to get it out of me, but I didn't want to believe Doran was my only hope. Milly didn't deal with demons; she wouldn't know what to do anymore than I did. Shit, I didn't want to believe Faris, to trust he was telling me the truth, but it wasn't looking like I had any choice.

O'Shea's arms tightened around me, then relaxed as he slid me into the back seat of his SUV. I tried to sit up.

"Lay down. Alex, here, get in beside her." A damp, but warm body pressed up against mine, his head resting on my legs.

I forced my eyes open. "I need to get warm, the venom . . ."

That was it, my strength was done.

4

"**A**damson?" He tried to wake her, but she was out, her face as white as the snow around them. "Shit."

He glanced around. "Alex, stay here." The werewolf did as he was told, and O'Shea went back to the flipped over Jeep and grabbed Rylee's bag of gear. No doubt she'd be wanting it when she woke up.

Tossing the bag into the passenger side, he slammed the door shut and got into the driver's seat. Training told him to wait on the paramedics that were on their way. He'd seen the skid marks and the grader driver had been freaking out on the side of the road, already calling for help. But Rylee's words were on repeat. He was a, more or less, by-the-books agent. Going off the rails to help her on the last case was a one-time deal for him.

A tap on his window stopped his flow of thoughts. It was the grader driver. O'Shea didn't bother to roll down his window. He had the heat cranked up in the hopes it would help whatever was going on with Adamson.

A wrinkled up face, partially covered by a dirty gray scarf, pushed against the window. "Hey, you can't take her with you! She was in an accident, man."

"I'm an FBI agent and I can take her into custody if I damn well want to." O'Shea snapped back, put the SUV into gear and put his foot on the gas pedal before he thought better of it.

Trust was not an easy thing for him, but he trusted Rylee's judgment, even in her half-frozen state. If she said all she needed was to get warm, then that was what he would do. One way or another, he would get her to trust him.

The snow continued to fall heavily, and with its deepening state whatever had a hold on Adamson continued to worsen. Her breathing laboured, and if it was possible, her face paled even more. O'Shea glanced over his shoulder as Alex whimpered and rubbed his face on her legs.

"Bad medicine."

"Alex, how warm is she?"

In the rear view mirror Alex tipped his head. This was not the time to have the werewolf not understand what he wanted. He simplified it.

"Is Rylee warm?"

Alex snuffled around for a moment. "No." Then he shook his whole body, rubbing his claws up and down his arms. "Cold. Icy queenie."

Shit.

He couldn't make the SUV any warmer. Already, he second guessed what he'd done, taking her away from the paramedics, hospitals, and the ability to have her warmed up medically.

She let out a groan. "Please. Don't hurt her."

"Adamson? I need you to wake up. Now!" O'Shea caught Alex cringe out the corner of his eye in the rearview mirror.

"No yelling." The werewolf whimpered.

How long would he have before she was past being able to help? At the next exit, he pulled off, searching for a place to get her warm.

The blinking lights of a cheap, cheesy motel flashed from out of the white blanket pulled over the world. *Good enough.* He skidded to a stop, the SUV sliding on the slushy snow. He stared up at the sign. It was one of Rylee's usual stops, one he'd followed her to more than once while trying to prove her guilt. Leaving the vehicle running, the heat on full blast, he ran to the motel door, stomping off the snow when he stepped inside.

O'Shea got a key from the motel clerk who was wearing a beat up old cowboy hat, his legs up on the registration desk.

"You got a dog too?" The old man asked, squinting out at the SUV, a large canine-like head clearly visible. Damn it all.

"Yes. Is that going to be a problem?"

The owner shrugged. "Long as he don't wreck anything. I only ever let one other person have their dog in here. She's a hell of a lot cuter than you though." Laughing, the old man shuffled around the edge of the desk. "Good day to hunker down. Ring me up if you need anything."

"Actually, have you got any salt?"

Lifting his eyebrows, the old man reached under the desk and O'Shea tensed. But all he brought out was a wooden salt shaker. "This do?"

"Yeah, thanks."

O'Shea shook his head and made his way back to the SUV, fighting the cold wind the whole way. After scooping Adamson up, and with Alex tight on his heels, he jogged to the room, lucky number 13. It looked as though it had been repaired recently. Shoving the door open, he hip-checked it shut behind them. The muted darkness felt muffled from the outside, snow falling steadily, blocking out much of the daylight.

After laying Rylee out on the bed, he put two fingers to her neck. Her pulse was irregular and barely discernible, not to mention her skin was ice cold and clammy. He strode to the thermostat and cranked it up full blast, then stripped off his trench coat.

"Alex, go turn the heat up in the bathroom." The werewolf bounded off, claws clacking on the linoleum when he hit it.

"Yuppy doody, gots it!"

Shaking his head, O'Shea took a deep breath. "I'm doing this to help you, Adamson." A large part of him was hoping she would wake up, give him hell, and then they could be off on their way. But no such luck.

Moving quickly, trying not to think about what he was doing, O'Shea stripped her down. He couldn't help it, but his eyes tracked the scars on her body. From the fresh one on her left arm, to the ones across her hips, stomach, and legs, he took it in. She had not had an easy life, yet still she fought to help others. And he'd been the ass standing in her way.

Again, focusing just on what needed to be done, he scooped her back into his arms. The shock of her nearly blue cold flesh could be felt through his shirt and set his heart hammering. "Come on, Adamson. Get mad at me. Yell. Give me something."

She was silent; her auburn hair a bright splash of color against her pale skin, the dark eyelashes against her cheeks a deadly contrast.

He carried her to the bathroom and cranked on the water, filling the tub while he cradled her. Using the water was the only thing he could think of; not just because it was warm, either. When he'd been spelled by the black Coven, Rylee had used water and salt to break it. Maybe this was the same?

"Alex, bring me the salt."

The werewolf did as he asked, even pouring it into the water for him, stirring it around with the tip of one claw before retreating with a frown on his face.

Instinctively, O'Shea stroked her hair. How could he not have seen her for what she was? For so many years, he'd accused her of murdering her own sister, blinded by his own ego to the point where he couldn't admit he was wrong.

When the tub was full, he slipped her body in, but she couldn't hold herself upright. Without another thought, he pulled her back out, stripped himself down to his shorts, and put her back in the tub. Shifting her forward, he slipped in behind her, and put one arm across her clavicle, the other around her waist. Already, the water and salt seemed to be doing the trick; her face pinked up and her eyelids fluttered.

"Liam." She whispered his name. He sat very still, suddenly aware of a large set of eyes watching him from the doorway. Frowning, golden, werewolf eyes. He frowned back.

"What?"

"Rylee mine. Not yours." Alex snapped his teeth at O'Shea then sat down in the doorway, continuing to glare at him.

If he hadn't been sitting in a tub of water, a naked woman in his arms and a serious problem with his body's reaction to the naked woman in his arms, he would have dealt with this. He'd had dogs before, knew that the minute they thought they were dominant you were in trouble. No doubt it was the same with werewolves.

Right.

Blissfully warm, I snuggled under the covers, recognizing the smell of my usual stop at John's motel. I didn't remember actually pulling in, the details of the last few hours were fuzzy. Stretching out, there was the familiar weight of a werewolf across my legs, but that wasn't what stilled my movements.

The hand resting on my hip, the deep breathing in my ear, and the rather distinct and unfamiliar feel of a large man pressed against my naked backside had me questioning what exactly had happened. I opened my eyes to see the still tattered curtains from our last visit giving me glimpses of the heavy snow falling. I felt like I was in some kind of weird time warp.

"You awake?" O'Shea's voice rumbled in my ear, the vibration from his chest against my back too pleasant by far.

I sat up fast, my head spinning. "Yeah. What the hell happened?" I clutched the blanket around my body, not shy, just feeling more vulnerable than I could have imagined without clothes and a weapon or two. Go figure.

O'Shea sat up, then leaned against the rickety headboard; a smile ghosted across his lips. "You don't remember?"

Staring at his broad, deliciously naked chest, I opened my mouth, but no sound came out.

The demon. Faris and Berget. The Jeep flipping over. It all muddled up inside my head; I groaned and shut my eyes. "My gear?"

"Got it."

I peeked out at him between the fingers of my one hand. Of all the men I had to go and lust after, it had to be one, the FBI agent who'd been after me for ten years, and two, Milly's current boy toy. Fuck me, I had bad taste.

The bed creaked and my eyes flew open, but O'Shea was just shifting his weight, crossing his legs. He was still wearing his pants at least. His dark eyes watched me carefully, but he didn't seem angry.

"Talk to me, Rylee. What's really going on?"

Come on, Rylee, be a grown up. Let him help you. I chided myself, knowing indeed, I did need his help now. At least until I could purge this venom out of my system.

"Apparently the demon we fought while rescuing India was a Hoarfrost demon. I got a sting from it." That was an understatement. "And now I am affected by the cold to the point of . . . ."

He finished for me, "Passing out."

I blew out a breath, not wanting him to know it could, in fact, kill me. Some things were better left unsaid. "Yeah. And I'm headed into Bismarck to meet up with a single mom."

"You need to take care of yourself before you go after a kid. You're no good to him or her in this kind of shape."

My arm muscles tightened, and I did my best to rein in my anger. He had, after all, saved my bacon. "I'm going after this kid. Now I know I just have to stay warm; there isn't an issue."

Snorting, he leaned forward, stomach muscles bunching into a perfect six-pack. I clamped my hands around the sheets, blood pumping at the sight of him.

He nodded. "I know better than to try and stop you."

"Good."

Dark eyes narrowed. "Which means you need to see how bad this really is. If you can walk from this hotel room to the SUV without shivering, then I'll help you go after this kid. Right now."

Oh no, he wasn't going to try and manipulate me, was he?

"And if I can't?" My voice was deadly soft.

"We take care of you first. Then come back for the kid."

I was already shaking my head. "No deal. I do this my way."

He stood up, looming over me, bare chest a serious distraction for my thoughts. "You almost died, because of cold weather that isn't even that cold. It's barely hovering around freezing. You can't go after this kid—"

"Don't tell me what I can and can't do! I didn't ask you to look out for me!" I forgot I was naked and rose to my knees on the bed.

We were nose to nose, screaming. Right back to the first day we'd met.

O'Shea put his hands on my shoulders, and then shoved me back onto the bed. "You are the most arrogant, delusional person I have ever met. You can't help this kid if you die. If you're dead, how many other kids are going to go unfound?"

God damn it, that hit below the belt.

"This could be a quick salvage, but I won't know that until I go see the mother." I was bargaining; I knew he had me. How had I lost control of this situation? The sheet slipped down further, baring even more skin to the open air. It wasn't cold, but a shiver traced through me as O'Shea's eyes dipped, widened and dilated.

The air between us all but crackled with tension. His jaw twitched and ever so slowly he lifted his eyes to mine.

"Wherever you go, I go too."

My teeth ached from gritting them. "Fine." I took great pleasure in seeing his eyes widen and his eyebrows climb with my agreement.

"You aren't going to argue with me?"

I shrugged in an attempt to act like I didn't care. "I will admit that I might need some help on this one, at least until I get the venom out of my system. It doesn't mean I'm agreeing to anything more."

O'Shea took a step back. "If this salvage turns out to be more than an easy find, we go get you the help you need. Deal?"

Everything I believed fought me on this. The kids always came first; they had to. Swallowing hard, I thought about how I had been unable to move, the cold paralyzing me. "Agreed."

As if he'd known my answer he gave a sharp nod of his head. "Let's get going then. There's still an hour or so left of light, enough to get where we need to go." He picked up his shirt where it hung over single chair in the room and walked to the bathroom, closing the door behind him. I glanced down at Alex who had remained surprisingly quiet throughout the whole exchange.

"You okay, Alex?" I reached over to touch his back, his fur warm under my hand.

Frowning, he rolled away from me with a grumble. "Hate stupid man with gun."

A burst of laughter I couldn't stop leapt out of me. "You hate him now?"

"Stupid man."

Although there were days I would have agreed with him, today was not one of them. I most likely owed my life to the FBI agent.

"Okay, that's all right. But he's coming with us. He's going to help us find a kid. So you be nice."

"I be nice. Nice with teeth."

Milly's words rang in my ears. Nope, that was so not going to happen. I had to nip this in the bud now. I grabbed Alex by the throat and he yelped as I first pulled him toward me, and then pinned him to the bed on his back.

"No teeth. Ever." I clenched my fingers around his neck, digging in. Amber eyes bugged out and fear quickly replaced the defiance that had been brewing. He flailed underneath me, the sheets tangling his legs, his claws catching my bare skin in places. I couldn't let up, not until we had this settled.

"Alex sorry!" He yelped, his voice a strangled cry, but he still fought me.

"Not good enough." I hated that I had to do this, but couldn't let him threaten people, because if he hurt someone, I would be the one who would have to end his life, and I didn't think I had it in me.

He finally went still, his whole two hundred pounds trembling underneath me. He could have killed me, but he was too submissive to even try.

"Rylee hate Alex."

"No, I don't hate you. I love you, Alex. That's why you have to be good."

Something shifted in his eyes. "You love Alex?"

"Yes, that's why you can't bite people. I don't want to lose you. You're my friend."

His lips trembled over his misshaped muzzle, and tears gathered up in his eyes. "Rylee like stupid man better than Alex."

Oh. My. God. I felt like he'd kicked me in the gut. Of course, he could scent things like desire and lust. I hung my head and lifted my hands from his neck. This was my fault. With the sheets tangled around us, I pulled him up into my arms and held him tight. His fur tickled my bare skin and the brush of his claws on my back only heightened my awareness of how much responsibility I truly had with him. In essence, he was a child trapped in a potential killer's body, one that I had to keep in line.

"No one will ever take your place, Alex. You will always be my wolf. Okay?"

He snuffled against my shoulder and glanced up at me. "Love Alex?"

"Yes, I'll always love Alex. No matter what."

A soft shuffle drew my eyes to the bathroom doorway where O'Shea stood, dressed and watching us. He cleared his throat.

"Your clothes are in the bathroom."

I nodded. "Thanks." Taking a sheet with me, I stood, my legs wobbly at first, and walked to the bathroom. I had to get my feelings for O'Shea under control. If not for myself, then for Alex.

5

My clothes were folded on the back of the toilet seat, my weapons on top. Gotta love a man that can fold clothes. *No, bad Rylee! No love for O'Shea!* If only it were that easy.

The bathroom was warm, but even so, my skin prickled with awareness. I had demon venom surging through me. Shit, what a way to start a salvage. While I dressed, I reached out with my abilities, brushing up against the venom. It was so cold it felt like it was burning, and I pulled back from it, tentatively trying a different approach. I didn't like things inside of me I couldn't understand, and I'd never before had to deal with something that felt like it was alive and crawling around in my body.

I tried to poke at it, but the thing was, the venom wasn't just a lump in my chest where I'd been stung, it was systemic, running through my veins as if it were a part of me. Like a colony of ants making my body their home. Shivering, I stared at the place I'd been stung, using my second sight to see the faint outline of a snowflake. It was lacy and black, and under any other circumstance I would have thought it was a cool tattoo.

As I slipped into my jacket, doing up the buttons, I pulled back my ability and left the venom alone. If Doran could truly help me, then so be it; while I didn't trust Faris, Berget had said the same thing. Go to Doran. I just had to hold it together long enough to get this kid.

I stepped out of the bathroom and Alex was sitting with his head on O'Shea's lap.

"I gave him a cookie," O'Shea said.

Smiling, I took a deep breath. "Glad you two boys are getting along."

Alex lifted his head and gave me a doggy grin, wagged his tail, and let out a fart. Grimacing, I headed for the door.

"I've got the SUV warming up, give it a minute," O'Shea said, but I was already out the door and heading for the front office, not even bothering to try his cell phone or mine. I needed space between us, and a moment to myself, even if it was just in John's office.

The wind and snow had picked up while I was out of it and all but howled around me. The venom coursing through me pulsed in time with the gusts of ice that yanked on my hair and clothes.

I jerked the door open to the manager's office and had to push it shut behind me, the wind was blowing so hard.

"Ry? What are you doing here? I didn't see your Jeep pull in," John said, his battered cowboy hat pushed back so he could see me.

"Yeah, I came in with a friend. Flipped the Jeep on the highway."

"Shit, you look not too bad for being flipped over."

I gave him a smile, my teeth chattering lightly just from that small exposure to the elements. Gods be damned, this was going to be more difficult than I thought. There had been a dim hope I could fight off the cold on my own now that I knew it was venom causing the problem; just tough it out. So much for that thought.

"Can I use your phone? I missed an appointment."

John waved me in. "Sure, phone's in the back." I scooted around the desk and into the inner sanctum of the office. Paperwork was neatly filed on one side; on the other it was piled in several spots. Mary, John's wife, was as tidy as they came. John, on the other hand, not so much. There was a small woodstove burning hot, keeping the storm at bay. I huddled as close to it as I could, the heat from the fire warming me considerably.

Under one of the piles, I found an older style rotary phone and a phone book. I looked up the bar, 'Bottom's Up,' and dialed.

The beat of the pounding music was the first thing I heard.

"Bottoms up, baby." Was the second sound that came through loud and clear.

"Hey, is Jewel there?" I fingered the curled cord of the phone around my hand.

"Yeah, she got stood up by some appointment, but she's still waiting."

"Tell her I'm on my way. The snowstorm sidelined me."

The guy grunted. "And you are?"

"Her appointment."

"Name?"

"Just tell her I'm on my way," I said, ending the conversation.

One more phone call to make. I dialed home, waited three rings, was almost on the fourth before Milly picked up with a sultry hello.

"Milly, what do you know about demons?" I asked softly, keeping my voice low. No need to freak John out.

I could hear her breathing, but she didn't answer. "Milly?"

"Why would you ask me that?"

"I just . . . ."

"Nothing, I know nothing about demons. Don't ask me questions like that!" She hung up before I could get in another question. Shit, so much for help from my best friend.

The door chimed and O'Shea's voice reached my ears. A rush of heat that had nothing to do with me standing next to the woodstove, and everything with thinking about being in bed naked with O'Shea, made me tingle all the way down to my toes. I *had* to get this desire under control. Taking slow even breaths, I thought about Milly and O'Shea in bed together, his broad chest under her hands, her long dark hair trailing around his face. Yup, that did it. Hurt and anger replaced the lust, and I stalked out to the main room, a glower on my face.

John stepped out of my way, smart man. "Take care, Ry."

"Thanks, you too, John."

I brushed past O'Shea and outside, running to the dark SUV waiting for me. Slipping into the front passenger seat, I slammed the door. At my feet was my bag of weapons and supplies, including my little black box. In the back Alex sat patiently, tracing designs in the fogged up windows with his claw tips. He seemed happier now, more relaxed. Maybe all he needed was reassurance that he wouldn't be ousted of his spot in my life. My fingers were crossed that was all it would take, but I doubted it. Werewolves were territorial, and if he'd decided I was part of his territory, even though I outranked him and he was ridiculously submissive, he would protect and defend me against anything to the death. Even against a human like O'Shea.

Speaking of the agent, he opened the driver's side, sat and quickly shut the door behind him, his eyes flicking over to me as he started up the SUV.

"Are you going to tell me where we're going?"

"'Bottoms Up.' You know it?" I batted my eyelashes at him. "What am I saying? You're a man, of course you know about the best stripper joint in town. I'll bet you don't even need directions."

The muscles in his neck flexed and he took a sharp breath in through his nose. His irritation was obvious to me, and I focused on it.

Driving the rest of the way into Bismark was, to say the least, awkward. I was doing my best not to think about how O'Shea's bare skin had felt against mine, but in the silence my mind kept wandering back. It was the agent who finally broke unspoken standoff.

"How do your clients find you?"

I started in my seat, his words jerking me out of my little fantasy world. "I have a middleman. He makes the initial contact, checks out the particulars, and then sends them onto me."

"Does this middleman have a name?"

I traced a sun on the fogged window beside me. "Charlie."

"Just Charlie?" O'Shea frowned, dark brows creasing downward. "You don't always charge the clients. So how do you pay the middleman, exactly?"

Okay, honesty being the best policy and all that shit . . . "I don't."

"What?"

I *so* did not want to explain, but we were too far away from 'Bottoms Up' to stall long enough to get out of this conversation. "My middleman wants to help. So he does. Whatever pay I make, he gets a small cut. If I chose not to charge, then he makes nothing. He's fine with that."

I could almost hear the gears grinding as O'Shea processed what I'd said. Thankfully, he didn't ask any more questions, and I went back to trying not to think about him.

Alex was the one to spot the strip joint before us through the dark and snow.

"Nipples!" He barked out, pointing with one claw to the pale neon sign shifting from a woman with her breasts covered, to not so much covered. Classy all the way.

O'Shea chuckled and I glared at him. The idea of seeing O'Shea ogle nude woman was too much like seeing him ogle Milly and made my anger spike.

"You two stay in here," I said as O'Shea parked the SUV in the closest parking spot.

Of course, Alex listened, but O'Shea ignored me and stepped out of the vehicle, matching my stride all the way to the front door. The cold whipped me as if I were buck naked, and the twenty second walk felt like I'd been out in the cold for hours. My fingers and toes were already numb. Shit, I needed to find this kid quick and get my ass into New Mexico and strangle Doran for whatever information I needed.

Lady Gaga's "Poker Face" pounded through the sound system and a quick glance at the stage showed me an interpretation I did not need. I looked away and came face to face with a barrel chest I didn't recognize, though he smelled familiar, a scent I couldn't quite put my nose on.

The bouncer was huge, towering over me and O'Shea, his arms at least the size of my upper body. If I didn't know better, I'd think he was an ogre, but there was no telltale hint of skin color that wasn't 'human.'

"No women allowed." He grunted, blocking my path.

"Fuck you, I'm here to see a client," I said, holding my ground.

The bouncer laughed, bald head glistening periodically as the strobe lights flicked our way. "You got a mouth on you, but I bet you don't know how to use it proper like." He licked his lips and gave me a wink that made me want to smash his face into my boot heel. O'Shea tensed beside me, shifting his weight from foot to foot. I gave him a look, you know the one that says, "Don't fuck this up man, I've got it." Jaw clenched, O'Shea gave me the barest of nods, though I could see he wasn't happy about me taking the lead.

Okay. I was done with the niceties. The bouncer may have been bigger than me, but there's always one surefire way to make a man crumple to the ground.

Outsmart him and then nail him.

"You know, for a big man, you sure are stupid. You see that guy over there, the one with the baseball hat?" I pointed behind him at nothing in particular, he turned to look and, using a chair for leverage, I jumped up and punched him in the side of the neck, dropping him to his knees. It might not sound like a really bad place to hit, but if you get the right angle there are tons of nerve endings travelling just under the skin there. Not to mention a lot of blood flow you can disrupt. In other words, it hurts like a son of a bitch. His hands went to his neck and I shoved him in the chest with my foot, toppling him backwards.

The music stuttered to a stop and I looked around to see we'd become the center of attention. Score one for me.

I raised my voice over the thumping music. "I'm here to see Jewel."

Multiple hands pointed to a painted black door that said "Dancers Only" on it. Leaving the bouncer writhing on the ground, I kicked his legs out of my way as I walked to the door. "Pussy."

O'Shea was right behind me, but said nothing until we were on the other side of the black door. "Excessive, don't you think?"

"No. Besides, you looked as ready to brawl as me."

He snorted. "You never tried that move with me."

"That one"—I thumbed back to the bouncer on the floor—"can't have me in handcuffs and thrown in jail." The hallway was brightly lit compared to the main area. It looked like each girl had her own dressing room, their names embossed in gold. Candy, Angel, Kitten, Sapphire. Gag me. None were even all that original. Finally we came to the end of the hallway, Jewel's name on the door.

I knocked softly. I didn't want to feel bad for the parents; it was hard enough going after kids without that added on. A soft, southern-accented voice answered.

"Come in."

Opening the door, I went in, O'Shea on my heels.

Jewel was stunning, her name suiting her perfectly. She wasn't wearing her stripper gear. Her dark blue jeans and peasant blouse had seen better days, but they were clean and cut to her size. Petite, barely five foot if I was guessing right, jet black hair and brilliant blue eyes that made me think of sapphires, were a stark contrast in pale, almost translucent skin. Like a miniature Elizabeth Taylor, minus the star power.

I pulled up the only extra chair and sat down. "I'm Rylee."

Her eyes welled up and she slumped onto a day bed tucked against the wall. "I thought you weren't going to come. My Ricky has been missing for two weeks."

Damn, she gave me his name already, not even waiting for me to ask. Some people just couldn't follow proper procedure. She was supposed to wait on me, let me decide if I was going to take the case on or not. If I was, I'd ask for the kid's name. Now there was no choice. I was in.

I frowned. "The police have given up already?"

O'Shea shook his head. "Two weeks, they wouldn't have stepped back. This isn't a cold case."

She shook her head, hiccupping back a sob. "No, they haven't. But I got this note, I was to give it to you."

A shiver of premonition rippled through me. This was not good, not good at all. I reached out and took a folded piece of paper that had smudges of dirt and some unidentifiable sticky mung I chose not to look too closely at.

> Stupid Tracker took my eyeball
> Now I hold something precious too.
> Find the boy quick or I'll kill him
> Instead of stupid you.

6

I handed the paper to O'Shea. There was only one creature whose eyeball I'd taken recently and not followed up with a kill.

"Is this who I think it is?" His fingers tightened on the note. A quick nod is all I gave him. No need for the client to realize it was my fault her boy was missing.

I leaned forward in my chair, a part of me wanting to tear my hair out. "I need a picture of Ricky, Jewel. I . . . we are going to find him." I lifted my eyes up to O'Shea. We should have killed that god damned Troll when we had the chance, but we'd been in such a hurry to get to India, we'd left him there handcuffed, missing one eye, but still very much alive. Mother-fucker, I was going to pull him apart piece by piece, starting with the eye he had left!

Jewel held out a picture, her hand trembling. The boy looked to be about thirteen or fourteen years old, the same coloring as his mom, down to the sapphire blue eyes.

"He's a good looking kid," I said.

"He's my whole world. I've already made the full deposit into your account. Please, please bring him back to me."

Her pain hit me like a hammer to the skull, pounding on me to let it in. She must have had some recessive psychic ability for me to feel so much from her. I blocked it out, focused on the picture, and sent out a thread of my Tracking ability to find the boy.

He was not close, a few hours in good weather, sleeping or sedated, I couldn't tell. But not dead.

"He's alive," I said, standing up and tucking the picture into my pocket. "Did Charlie give you the rundown? The rules? No police, no phone calls."

She nodded, then reached out and clasped my hands. "Yes, please, please just bring him back to me."

Her grief hit me again, the touch of her skin on mine making a connection I did not want. I pulled away from her and looked up at O'Shea. "We've got to go."

"I'll pray for you, all of you." Jewel looked to me first, then to O'Shea. Always with the prayers. I wasn't sure they helped, but every parent I'd ever met gave them.

The room was full of emotions I struggled to fight off. I almost ran to the door, flinging myself out and gulping in a large breath of air.

O'Shea shut the door behind us. "The AA division does not approve of what we are about to do. I can't have this on record."

Taking one last deep breath and tying myself off to Ricky so I would know the second his status changed, I headed toward the exit. "And what do you think we're going to do, exactly?"

"Do I need to say it?"

I thought about it. "Yes. Because I don't want there to be any illusions."

"We're going to find the kid and kill the Troll."

Smiling, I put my hand on the door out to the bar, opening it before I answered him, and again the place went quiet.

A quick glance around showed me the bouncer had buggered off. Good. The last thing I needed was a bad ass trying to prove himself.

There was a flash of movement, faster than any human I'd ever met, and a set of hands grabbed me from the side, lifting me high into the air. With my arms pinned, there wasn't much I could do but kick and scream. I settled for kicking, swinging the back of my boot heel first into the bouncer's ear. He roared with anger and I hoped a lot of pain, but didn't let go.

There was a swirl of movement and the bouncer went still. As if he'd been turned into stone. Not so impossible in my line of work. From what I could see, O'Shea had a rather large knife resting just under the bouncer's jaw. It looked like one of mine I'd left behind in the root cellar. Good, at least it would be spelled to cut deep and fast.

O'Shea adjusted his stance; it would allow him a clean, fast cut. "Put her down." His voice was as cold as the weather outside. The bouncer did as he was told, only he threw me at O'Shea, sending us both crashing to the floor. I kicked out behind me in the air blindly, and caught something on the bouncer. It felt like his upper thigh. Grabbing for my sword handle, I got my blade out in time to follow the kick with a swing of my sword that bit through his belly. He flailed backwards, hands over his guts. I didn't want to kill anyone; that wasn't my game. But he wasn't exactly human. I just hadn't figured out quite *what* he was.

I got to my feet, brushing my clothes off. "I tried to be nice, tried to keep this simple. But you are *really* pissing me off."

The bouncer grimaced at me, a bare flash of his teeth . . . ah, now I understood why he was giving us such problems.

I crouched down beside his face, placing the edge of my sword across his throat, let the pressure of the blade split his skin through to blood. He swallowed and rolled large, amber eyes up to mine. He was a strong one to be able to shift back and forth, to hide right under the human's noses.

"If I know what you are," I whispered. "Then you must know what I am."

One blink of those wolf-like orbs satisfied me as a yes.

My lips were almost against his ear. "Since you're here, and I'm here." I took a deep breath, recognizing the wolf musk for what it was now. "Take a message to your bitch for me."

He let out a growl and I put a bit of pressure on the blade, felt it rest up against his esophagus. "Tell her if she keeps hounding my wolf, I will start a new business and add Hunter to my resume."

I stood, wiped my blade on his torn shirt, and then strode to the door, glancing over my shoulder at O'Shea who stood there a tad bit wide-eyed. Of course, he didn't know the bouncer would be just fine. "He's one of Alex's old friends. He'll be peachy keen in no time."

Understanding dawned on his face. "Same ones who tried to kill him last month?"

The bouncer squirmed on the floor.

"Yup. Same ones."

O'Shea said nothing more, just made his way to my side and we left 'Bottoms Up.'

I ran to the SUV and piled in, rubbing my arms. If the bouncer/werewolf had tried anything outside, there was no way I'd have been able to fight him. Again, the short exposure to the cold was all it took to numb my fingers and toes, and even though O'Shea cranked the heat up, my teeth were chattering.

Alex took one sniff of me and recoiled as if I'd slapped him.

"No, no, no. Stinky, bad wolf." He started to rock in his seat, weaving his upper body back and forth, whimpering in between words.

"Rylee, we have to go," O'Shea said.

"I know, just give me a minute." I was climbing into the back to soothe Alex, his eyes almost rolling back in his head with fear.

"No, I mean we have to go now." He threw the SUV into gear and hit the reverse while I tried to calm the freaked out werewolf in the backseat.

"What the hell?" I yelped, crashing into the back-seat. "You aren't helping!"

"The bouncer had friends."

I whipped around in my seat to see a half dozen 'friends' swarm out the doors of the strip joint and shift into wolf form. Unlike Alex, who was trapped between human and wolf, these werewolves were strong enough for a full shift in either direction. The wolf part of them was far oversized compared to a natural wolf. They were at least five feet at the shoulder and around four hundred pounds. Fast, lean predators. Six of them; shit we were in trouble.

"Go, go, go!" I shouted. "They can rip open this SUV like a tin can."

O'Shea put the SUV into gear and hit the gas, fish-tailing in the snow. Out the back window, the pack was gaining on us, their claws digging into the hard-packed snow, where our tires struggled for traction. Alex cowered in the back seat, claw-tipped hands covering his head.

It was like watching a bad horror flick up close and personal, the size of the werewolves making it feel like I was watching them in a rear view mirror, 'Objects may be closer than they appear.'

If we crashed we were dead, either by werewolf or vehicular manslaughter. "Can you go any faster?"

"Not unless you want another flipped vehicle. It's too slick." He barely got the words out before we were slammed from behind, the screech of claws on metal tearing at my ears. The werewolves were peeling the SUV like a banana. Shit, I had to slow them down.

Grabbing my bag of gear, I pulled out my little black box. Inside was an array of pre-made spell bombs Milly had put together for me. I grabbed the green one and cracked the hard shell to reveal the true bomb inside. Encased in a balloon, it would break on contact, spreading to everything in the vicinity. Simple and effective.

Holding it carefully, I crawled over to the back seat. There were holes in the back of the SUV that had not been there moments before. This was not good on so many levels. The wind howled in, freezing up my body even while my heart pumped hard with adrenaline.

"Roll down the back window."

"Are you crazy?"

"Trust me."

I waited, poised for the one moment I would have. I could see all six of the pack members, bunched together as they prepped for their next leap. The window went down, and the pack leapt as a unit. I threw the spell-bomb and yelled the ignition word.

"*Abrogate!*"

A flash of green lit the air behind us and the pack was thrown backward, landing in a heap as still as death. The spell would keep them away from us for at least ten minutes, plenty of time to get the hell out of Dodge.

"Window!"

It wound up, clicked shut, and while some of the wind was blocked, it was still not warm enough. Alex snuffled up against me and I slid my arms around him. His body vibrated with fear, but he was like a large, heated blanket.

"Rylee, what the hell was that?" O'Shea asked.

"One of Milly's spells. It repels things."

"Shit."

I couldn't help feeling proud of Milly. "Most witches can't repel a mosquito with that spell; it's complex and draining to make. Milly's been making them since she was seventeen."

"Remind me to thank her."

I grunted and buried my face into Alex's fur, breathing in the scent of home. No way was I going to remind O'Shea of anything that had to do with Milly. Call me childish if you want, but I didn't have to help them get along. I wouldn't stand in their way, but I wasn't going to throw them a freaking party.

"I need you to talk to me." O'Shea said, his voice sounding further away than it should have.

"Why?"

"So I know you're still with me."

I shivered, a blast of cold curling around my face. "This shouldn't be happening."

Lifting my eyes up, I caught his look in the rear view mirror. "Why not, you were stung by a demon?"

"I'm an Immune, someone who can't be affected by venom, bites, nothing. This is impossible." I started to shake. Alex curled around me, sheltering me from the cold only I seemed to be able to feel. O'Shea slipped out of his long trench coat as he drove and handed it back to me. It was still warm from his body and his cologne hung heavy on it. Wrapping the coat around me, I warmed up considerably. I wanted to believe it wasn't because of the sudden rush of hormones racing through my system. Just from a single sniff of cologne? Gods be damned, I was in trouble.

"So, what else could it be?"

I didn't answer him, because I didn't know. Instead, I focused on the kid, Ricky, felt him pull me to the side, his life force an easy beacon. "Turn left."

O'Shea cranked the wheel to the right, heading toward the interstate. "We are not going after this kid yet."

I sat up, bracing myself against the cold. "I said turn left! The kid is the other way."

"You can't go after him, not like this. You said you could get help in New Mexico, so that's where we're going."

My jaw dropped and I struggled to understand that O'Shea had just hijacked my plans. Shivering, my body was shaking so hard I couldn't even still my fingers enough to lock my seatbelt around me.

"Turn around, O'Shea. Kid first," I said through chattering teeth.

He shook his head, and I wanted to hit him. "You'll pass out in the next few minutes, and then we'll go where I say we're going."

"Son of a bitch," I yelled, trying to use my anger to fuel me, to gain enough energy to prove I could deal with this. The burst of anger did nothing but seem to drain me more, and I slumped into my seat, head lolling against Alex.

"You're an asshole," I mumbled as unconsciousness pulled me under again.

As soon as Adamson passed out, O'Shea pulled over. Leaving the SUV running, he grabbed the repair kit from the backseat and pulled out the duct tape. In a few short minutes, he had the holes patched over, blocking almost all of the wind. What was she thinking? There was no way she could face down a troll, or more werewolves, or anything as long as this cold weather was hitting her as it seemed to be. Why couldn't she see it?

"Damn it, she's not Wonder Woman." The wind swirled his words away, and he took a slow breath to calm himself. He knew why she did it, knew it better than most. The drive to save missing children, to return them to their families was nigh on an obsession with her. She needed it as much as she needed food and air.

The snow slid out from under his feet, the temperature making it a wet, slushy mess rather than the usual dry cold. It was going to make driving a supreme pain in the ass. Sliding back into the driver's seat, he reached back to Adamson, and slid a hand under the coat he'd tossed her. While she wasn't toasty warm, she also wasn't frosted over like when he'd found her in the Jeep.

"Adamson, you awake?"

She grumbled something and snuggled deeper under the coat and closer to the werewolf, who was now giving him the stink eye. Amber eyes glared at him, narrowing as the elongated jaw dropped open.

"Stop touching." He growled, pushing O'Shea away. Knowing it probably wasn't the smartest thing, he said what was on his mind.

"You and me, we're going to have a chat soon." His voice was steady, though his heart was suddenly pounding. "And you are not going to like it. Buddy."

Alex snorted and waved at him, as if to dismiss the agent.

Putting the SUV into gear, making sure the heat was cranked up as hot as it could go, sweat beading up on his skin, he pulled back onto the road, heading for the interstate.

Eyes focused on the road, he almost didn't hear the ring of his cell phone buried in the console. Yanking it out and answering, he almost wished he hadn't.

"O'Shea, this is Agent Valley. Where the hell are you?"

Right, his boss didn't know about this little trip.

"Uh, I'm with Adamson. We are . . ."

Agent Valley laughed. "Tell me you aren't in bed with her. When I said partner, I meant working partner; you know that, right? 'Cause if you're in bed with her, I can't guarantee you won't get busted down to traffic. I mean it. We need her on this division and if you mess it up because you can't keep your hands off her, I will have your ass in a sling."

O'Shea' let out a slow breath. "I understand, sir. And for the record, that hasn't ever crossed my mind." *Yeaaaah, only about every other minute.*

"Then, what, pray tell are you doing?"

"Trying to convince her to trust me, to work with me."

There was silence for almost a full minute before Agent Valley came back on. "Fine. Do what you have to do, but make it happen. We have problems here. A god damned Harpy was sighted flying south. A Harpy. Of all the God damned things we need right now, this is not one of them!"

A distinct desire to close his eyes and lay his head on the steering wheel hit O'Shea. He settled for tightening his grip on the faux leather grips of the wheel. "Understood, sir. I should be back in North Dakota in a few days."

"What?" The ice in Agent Valley's voice could rival the cold hammering the outside of the SUV.

"Sorry, sir, you're breaking up." O'Shea hit the end button, then turned off the phone completely.

"Fuck, this is bad."

From the backseat, Alex echoed him, though O'Shea thought it was twisted to be directed back at him, amber eyes watching him closely.

"Fuck is bad."

"Yeah, that about sums it up," O'Shea muttered as he pulled onto the interstate and headed south.

Heading out of town, dodging the various spin outs, navigating the winter storm, the SUV was silent except for Alex humming to himself next to me. I was awake now, warmed up to the point of being with it again, but I was trying to stay inconspicuous. The thing was, I knew O'Shea was right; I was in no shape to go after Ricky, not in this weather with demon venom pumping through me. That didn't make me any happier about the situation.

I stared out the window as the sun set, darkness putting us into a world that looked like we were the only people left on the planet. The snow swirled down around us, cutting us off from the rest of the world, muffling sound and light.

"Where are your parents now?"

O'Shea's voice startled me out of my nearly hypnotized state. How the hell had he known I was awake?

I crunched lower into my seat. "I don't know. I haven't seen them since—" I didn't want to go back to that time in my life. It was dark and ugly.

He glanced back at me, and I curled up tighter. This was not a discussion I wanted to have with anyone, certainly not O'Shea. So I turned it back on him.

"Where are your parents?"

"Dead."

Good job, Rylee, real good job.

"I'm sorry. I didn't know." Lame, but what else did you say to that kind of confession? Maybe it would put an end to the conversation.

"Not your fault. They died right before I finished my four-year degree."

Crap, looked like the agent wanted to talk. I squirmed in my seat, and didn't answer him. Personal stories were not my forte. I didn't like sharing mine, and I didn't particularly like hearing other people's. It was awkward; I never knew what to say. Shit happens, get over it. People didn't like to hear that. Hell, I wouldn't like to hear that, but it was the truth as far as I was concerned.

His hands shifted on the wheel and he stared out the windshield for a moment. I thought perhaps he was getting the drift. No such luck.

"They were killed, both of them, by a serial shooter. He was targeting 'well-to-do' couples to get back at his employers for laying him off. They were in the wrong place at the wrong time."

I kept my mouth shut.

Alex shifted in the back, and then stuck his head onto the middle console. "Bad guns?"

Shut up! I wanted to shout, but I satisfied myself with closing my eyes; acting uninterested. The biggest problem? I wanted to know more about him, which was exactly why I needed to pull back.

He was with Milly, my BFF. Right. Which was why thinking about him as anything but a tool to help me get the salvage done was a bad idea.

O'Shea's deep voice spilled over me, as he spoke to Alex, like I wasn't even there. He talked about growing up on a small farm in Kentucky, about going away to college, how he hadn't wanted to be an FBI agent until the death of his parents.

"What were you studying in university?" The question popped out of me before I could stop it.

O'Shea glanced over at me. "Art. I was in taking my Bachelor of Arts program."

I could actually see him as a sculptor, hands working with clay as he molded shapes out of a lumpy substance. It was far too easy to imagine him shirtless and creating something amazing. Yes, far too easy. I had to say something. Something that would stop this from going any further.

"What the hell, how did you get to be a goddamn FBI agent from a fruity art student?"

His mouth tightened. "I was not a fruity art student. I was studying—"

"Nooooo, you were a freaking hippy turned into a gun toting agent. You can't tell me you had that planned? I mean, I can't believe the FBI even let you in!" Once I got going, I couldn't stop myself. There had to be space between us. Had to be. Inwardly I cringed, but didn't stop.

"They require a degree," he ground out, fingers tightening on the wheel, vein pulsing in his neck. "They don't care what degree; it just has to be a four-year degree."

Forcing a laugh, I clutched at my belly. "Are you kidding me? Sheesh, here I thought I'd had a real agent chasing me all those years."

It was his turn to play the silent role, and I slumped down in my seat and flung an arm over my eyes. It wasn't nice what I'd said, I knew that. But what the hell, we weren't playing truth or dare. I hadn't asked him to spill his guts.

More than that, I had to stop this attraction. I had to find a way to push him out of my life for good. Because every time he touched me, every time I looked his way and caught a glimpse of heat in his dark eyes, the intensity of what I was feeling increased. Next thing, I'd be throwing myself bodily at him and begging for him to do more than kiss me.

"You can be a real bitch, Adamson."

"I know, Liam." I whispered, rolling my back to him and shutting my eyes.

It was going to be a long drive to New Mexico.

7

She'd whispered his name, just that, so simple and it undid him all over again. Damn, the woman could be more mercurial than the weather. Even so, he'd seen her put up her guard, watched her back away from a conversation that was anything more than surface. And now she was feigning sleep to avoid him. He reached over and shook her shoulder, though he knew she wasn't really asleep.

"What's the plan, when we get to New Mexico?"

Twisting in her seat, she lifted an eyebrow. "No plan. Go in, strangle some information out of Doran, get the venom out of me. Done, time to go home."

They were driving through South Dakota and would soon be crossing into Wyoming, but it seemed as if the storm was following them.

"Sounds like all of your ideas," he paused for effect, feeling a need to knock her down a peg or two. "Stupid and naive."

She sucked in a sharp breath of air. Good, at least he had her attention now. If she wanted to play hardball, fine by him.

"You ass, what do you know about going after anything supernatural?"

"I know you should have at least an *idea* of a plan. Maybe even something for a back up." He yelled, angrier than he'd been in a while; since he'd decided Adamson was someone he wanted for a partner, and that was all she could ever be.

Rylee slumped into her seat, closed her eyes as thunder rumbled the entire SUV. Sitting up straight, she stared out into the swirling snow.

"Did you feel that?"

Oh, shit, he had a bad feeling about this. "Yes. Thunder."

"No, not thunder." Her eyes scanned the darkness and snow. She pointed ahead of them. "Just try to avoid them, they aren't going to cause us any problem, but if you hit one then we'll be in trouble."

He strained his eyes, leaning forward. "What are you talking about?"

A large, white, furred body slid out from in front of them, the fur tipped with silver highlights not unlike Alex's coat, but other than that he couldn't tell what he was looking at.

He fought not to hammer on the brake, knowing it would send them into a spin. "What are they?"

Rylee crawled over the console and into the front seat, buckling herself in.

She smiled, and it lit up her face. "I think I'll make you guess. But don't worry, as long as we don't bother them, they won't bother us."

He slowed down, blinking several times as one large, furred, almost human body came fully into view. Human in shape, not in size, the thing was fifteen feet or better in height. It grinned down at

him and his mind struggled to put the pieces together.

Yeti, bigfoot, abominable snowman. The creature
towered over the SUV, and it blended in so well with
the surrounding area it made his eyes water to stare at
it. The way it moved was like nothing he'd ever seen,
as if it were a part of the elements, blending into the
snow and the wind.

"It's a part of their camouflage. If I hadn't pointed
them out, you never would have seen them. Like so
much of the supernatural, you humans have no idea
what you're looking at most of the time, or write off
what you see as a trick of the eyes." She waved up
at one of the creatures and it grinned down at her,
waving back. Alex got excited, hopping up and down,
finally managing to roll down a window.

"No, Alex, it's too cold," O'Shea barked, thinking
about the loss of heat for Adamson.

Her fingers stole over his bicep, gripping it lightly,
and she shook her head. "It's okay, I'm still warm."
The heat from her skin on his shot through him,
straight to his groin, at the thought of those fingers
sliding other places. Rylee seemed amused at his total disbelief; the anger in the air draining away from
them both as they watched the large creatures dance
in the snow.

Alex hung halfway out the window, howling and
waving at the creatures as they thumped around, their
heavy footsteps sounding like distant rolls of thunder.

"There is no way we could miss them, they're too
huge, and they leave footprints," O'Shea said, just as
they left the . . . herd . . . of creatures behind.

"You think creatures like that haven't learned how to hide their passing? Come on, O'Shea, they aren't mindless. They think like you and me, like Dox and Alex. Just because they're supernatural doesn't mean they're stupid."

She snorted; Alex pulled himself back in and pressed the window button delicately with the tip of one claw. "Fuuuuuunnnnnnnyyyyyy!" He howled, hopping up and down.

O'Shea tightened his grip on the steering wheel. "Anything else I should expect, in the way of creatures?"

Rylee smiled over at him, a distinct twinkle in her eye. "Oh, Mr. Agent man, you ain't seen nothing yet."

Great, just fantastic. More creatures than he could identify, a werewolf in his backseat howling at the top of his lungs, a woman he was as confused about as he'd ever been, and snowstorm that wouldn't let up.

This was going to be some trip.

We rolled to a stop on the outskirts of New Mexico, right in front of the welcome sign. O'Shea leaned forward and put his head on the steering wheel, a tired sigh escaping him. "Please tell me that doesn't mean what I think it does."

I glanced up at the big billboard sign. "The Land of Enchantment. What, you never read the sign before?"

"Tell me it doesn't mean we are stepping into. . ."

The smile that spread across my lips went unnoticed by him. "A land full of enchantment and the supernatural? You bet. Look, the agent can learn things."

I clapped my hands together and Alex mimicked me, clapping his big mitts together over and over.

O'Shea let out a groan. "Can you drive?"

"I thought you'd never ask." We switched spots, me climbing over the seats so I wouldn't have to go outside. While New Mexico was hot as hell in the summer, the winters could be just as bad, even worse than those in North Dakota. O'Shea and I swapped and a flurry of ice filled wind snaked into the SUV before we could stop it. The storm front must have been covering a larger area than we thought. At least I hoped that was all we were dealing with. I wanted Faris to be wrong. I wanted to believe what the Hoarfrost demon had stuck me with wouldn't cause all this bad weather following us around. All the way through Wyoming and Colorado we'd been chased by the snow, only a few spots were clear and those quickly disappeared.

Rubbing my arms, I buckled up, and headed for Dox's place, my mind whirling with possibilities. My plan was to drop Alex and O'Shea off, then head to Doran's on my own. No need for the daywalker Shaman to realize he could have collateral in my friends.

Speaking of friends, The Landing Pad was a pub and hotel run by one of the few I could call friend, a blue-skinned ogre that seemed to be waiting for us, if him standing on the front stoop of the pub was any indication. We pulled in and he was scooping me into his arms before I could fully get out of the SUV.

"Rylee, this is bad, so bad. I didn't think you were coming."

I felt a twinge of guilt. I hadn't come for him, but now that I was here, I would do my best to help him in the time I had.

Alex scrambled to get out, yelping about brownies, scratching the shit out of the leather seats in the process. I distantly wondered if O'Shea was going to catch hell for the deep gouges.

"Hey, Dox." The ogre put me down, the rings in his nose, lips, and eyebrows winking at me. One day I'd have to ask him why he had none in his ears.

A sharp intake of air turned my head. O'Shea was staring at us, eyes wide. What was his problem now?

"Adamson, you forgot to mention Dox wasn't human." He said, his voice controlled, but not altogether steady.

Oh, that was the problem. Right. Now that O'Shea knew what he was looking at, Dox's method of hiding what he was wouldn't work anymore.

"Dox, meet Agent O'Shea. Again," I said, indicating they should shake.

Dox reached over and took one of O'Shea's hands in his, engulfing it completely. "O'Shea, try not to diss my place again. It'll go badly for you this time."

Ogres and subtlety, like oil and water. He made me smile.

I cleared my throat. "Inside." I strode for the doors, fighting the urge to buckle under the cold. My reaction to the weather seemed to be getting worse each time. Not a good sign.

Dox started in on the questions right away. "Do you think you can Track Louisa? And why is there a Harpy in my back yard?"

How did I tell him Louisa was second on my list of salvages when I was here? I reached for Ricky, and though he was very distant, I could feel his life force. Still good, and still sleeping. That was a bit of a concern. Had they drugged him to keep him quiet? It was possible. We had to hurry, I couldn't be here long.

"Harpy first." I glanced around the room. "Dox, you got anything that will keep me warm?"

He pointed to a heavy hunk of fur hanging off a hook. "Buffalo robe should do it. Those things will keep the worst weather out, better than any man-made crap you'll buy from a store."

The robe smelled like a mixture of booze, smoke, and licorice. Slipping it on, I shifted under it. It had to be over twenty-five pounds, but already my body was warming up under it, a perfect barrier to the cold.

Jogging to the back of the motel, I could see Eve was in fine form, dozing in the sunshine in spite of the cold temperature. Her head bobbed up as we rounded the corner.

"Rylee! You're here already. I thought you would be longer." She cocked her head to one side.

"Complications." I said.

"Is there anything I can do to help?"

Clinging to the robe, I fingered the inner lining, feeling the nicks where the animal had been skinned, while I debated how much to tell her at this point. I had to go see Doran, and that I would need to do alone. A hip bumped into mine and I dropped a hand onto Alex's head. This was stumbling block number one. O'Shea moved up to flank me on the other side. And there was stumbling block number two. Call it a hunch, but I had a feeling Doran wouldn't be all that helpful if O'Shea was hovering, or if I had a werewolf at my heels.

"Yes, I think so. O'Shea, would you take Alex inside?"

"Why?"

Shit, what a good question. "For brownies."

I gave Dox sideways look he caught with ease. He would be the only one not to stand in my way. Alex started to squeal, his body shaking, "Browniiiiieeeesss! YAY!"

O'Shea took me by the arm and stared down at me. "Give me the keys."

I pulled the SUV keys out of my pocket and dropped them into his hand. "Here. See? I just want to talk to Eve for a minute." Keeping my eyes wide and innocent, I knew the agent could see through my charade. The thing was, he had no idea what I was up to. Perfect.

Clenching the keys tights, he backed up. "I'll give you some room, but I'm not letting you out of my sight. You shouldn't be on your own right now."

Dox watched the back and forth between us, finally pursing his lips. "Well, I'll take the werewolf inside, let you two have your little lovers spat on your own."

I gasped, shocked that not only would Dox so quickly see my hang ups, but that he would air them out.

"We are not—"

"That isn't what's going on," O'Shea said. "She's got some demon venom pulsing through her, and it makes her vulnerable."

"Hey! Keep your mouth shut," I yelled, striding over to him, jamming one finger into his chest, then lowering my voice. "You need to learn when not to speak, Agent. There is more than one bad ass supernatural out there that would like to see me dead and buried in an unmarked grave."

He blanched. "I thought you were safe here with your friend."

"Dox would never do anything. But that doesn't mean there aren't others around. There are those that can hear things without being seen, and then would sell the information." I let out a breath. "Go inside, don't drink the ogre beer, and I'll be done in a bit."

Apparently, my spat of anger did it. The three males who were so very different in so many ways, disappeared back into the motel, two with heads lowered, one with a tail tucked between his legs. I buried my face into the robe, and took a deep breath.

Eve scratched at her head with one talon. "You carry demon venom?" Her voice was low; at least she listened when I said to be quiet.

"Yes," I said, my mind already skimming ahead to what I was going to have to do.

She ruffled her feathers. "I knew I smelled demon on you. When you woke me up."

My jaw dropped. Eve had known before I had, she just hadn't known what it was. Shit, I was going to have to listen more to her.

Lowering her head to mine she whispered, "What is it, Rylee? You have never before asked for my help."

I took in her size, knowing she could easily pick up and carry away creatures half her size for a meal. But would she carry me?

"Eve, you could pack me, couldn't you?"

She stopped her scratching and turned large round eyes on me, her voice lowering conspiratorially. "You want me to fly you somewhere?"

I nodded. "Yes. If you are able to."

Clacking her beak, she hopped around, her delight obvious. "I thought you'd never ask!"

With a quick look over my shoulder, I made sure all three of the guys were inside. Shadows moved in the window, good enough for me.

"Best place will be ahead of my wings, Rylee. You can grip my feathers, or wrap your arms around my torso. It won't hurt me."

I licked my lips. "Okay, any other tips?"

"Don't fall off, I'm not sure I will be able to catch you fast enough, I am no dragon." Her voice was dead serious.

"Should I be worried about . . . dragons?" I thought they'd been banished to Europe. In fact, I was sure they had; it had happened not long after I'd met Giselle.

Eve ruffled her feathers. "They encroach from time to time, but I have only seen one. I doubt we will have a problem." Her voice rose in excitement. "Where are we going?"

I pushed thoughts of dragons from my mind and shoved my hands deep into the pockets, tried to look casual. It was as if I could feel when O'Shea was watching me, his eyes burrowing into my shoulder blades. "I'm going to sidle up to you, and then as soon as I jump up, you take off. Got it?"

She gave me a smile, wrinkles forming at the corners of her beak. "Is it a dangerous mission?"

"Not for you."

The smile slipped from her face. "You would protect me still. I wish to learn to fight, not be coddled."

This had to be one of the top ten strangest conversations I'd ever had. "You can fight, I promise, just not this time. If you want to help, you can act as if you would like to hurt him. You know, intimidate him." That seemed to mollify her. "Now, are you ready?"

She bobbed her head and stretched her wings. "I am ready."

O'Shea's voice called out from the motel. "Ready for what?"

I sprinted for Eve, gathering the thick coat around me, knowing I would only have one shot at this. She crouched when I reached her side, coiling up in order to launch into the air. Grabbing a handful of feathers, I jumped, throwing a leg over her back as if I was mounting a horse. Before my butt even landed, Eve sprung into the air, her wings outstretched, the downdraft swirling around a furious O'Shea.

"Adamson!"

I cupped one hand around my mouth, the other clinging tightly to the rising Harpy. "I told you not to call me that."

Anything else he said was lost as Eve and I rose into the air above the Landing Pad. Clinging to Eve, I hoped I would be able to hang on the whole way. Even with the buffalo jacket tucked around me, the cold seeped through, icing over my limbs inch by inch. The heat radiating off Eve's body and up through my legs helped, but I was still frigid as we rose higher into the colder air. With a shaking hand, I pointed, directing her to Doran's place. The daywalker was about to get a visit he couldn't see coming in a thousand years.

I was wrong; he not only knew we were coming, he was waiting for us.

8

We landed in Doran's courtyard, slipping through the Veil in order to do so. From the road, to any human eyes, all that would be seen was a vacant lot for sale, run down and littered with junk. The reality was Doran, Shaman and daywalker, had a swanky place complete with Koi pond, fountains and a large courtyard with a perpetually burning fire pit. But it was all hidden behind the Veil, kept from prying human eyes. Here was a doorway into the supernatural not many people ever experienced.

The Daywalker stood next to the fire pit, lifting a hand to us as we landed. White-blond hair tipped in black, piercings above one eye and the corner of his bottom lip, and green eyes that could rival Milly's for pristine beauty.

We landed with a soft thud, Eve's wings not even stirring the fire. Interesting, but that wasn't why I was here.

"Rylee, I thought you would be here sooner," Doran said, taking my hand as I slid off Eve. I jerked my fingers away.

"Don't touch me."

He looked truly shocked. "I thought we were friends now. Don't tell me you're upset about last time?"

Last time I'd needed his help, he'd attacked me, then tried to be-spell me. Yeah, to say I was still pissed would be accurate.

Eve leaned forward. "May I eat him now?"

Doran's eyes widened and the daywalker paled; I had to fight back a grin.

"You would use a Harpy against me?"

"Only if you misbehave," I said. "As it is right now, I need your help, and you're going to give it to me."

Smiling, the Shaman turned and beckoned me to a seat across the fire pit. "I am always willing to help, for a price, of course."

I was already shaking my head. "Nope, not this time. Faris sent me to you." I didn't mention Berget; I doubted her name would have the same effect as the vampire's. I was right.

Doran sank into his chair and I could see him swallow, watched the blood drain from his face. "Faris, how . . . how do you know him?"

Gratified by the fact the vampire's name meant something to Doran, I was bothered it scared him so badly. I slumped into the chair across from the daywalker/Shaman, scooting it closer to the fire, hugging the buffalo robe around me.

"He tried to kill me when I went after India. And he paid me a visit yesterday." I propped my boots up on the edge of the fire pit, soaking up the heat from the flames. The flight with Eve had accomplished me getting here, but shit, I could barely feel my skin. The wind in the upper stratosphere was brutally cold.

Doran tugged at his lip ring, his eyes distant. "I do not know what I can do to help you with a vampire. He is stronger than me."

I laughed. "I don't think anyone can help me with him. I need you for something else."

He lifted his eyes to mine. "You are looking for Louisa, yes?"

"No." I let out a sigh. "I have some bad ass venom running through me. I need to purge it. And it seems to be getting worse, not fading as I hoped it might."

His eyebrows lifted, the rings in the one catching the firelight. "Wait, that's impossible. You are an Immune."

"You think I don't know that?" I snapped, slamming my boots into the rough tile of the fire pit. "Why the hell do you think I'm here, to have tea and biscuits and a lively discussion?"

Eve snickered. "Now may I eat him?"

I glared at the daywalker. "Not yet."

He acted as though the Harpy wasn't looming over him. "Hmm. How did the venom get into you?"

"When I was trapped in a pentagram with the demon," I said, fingering the blade handle tucked against my side, remembering the moment as if I were there again. "I jumped into the pentagram to get India out, and the demon slammed its stinger into my physical body."

Doran leaned forward. "You mean that it wasn't physically present, but a spirit demon still?"

I thought for a moment. "Yes, that sounds right. Will that make a difference?"

He shrugged, threw something into the fire; I watched as silver sparkles danced upward on the heat. "It will change how we draw the venom from you. From what you are saying, I believe it will continue to worsen until either it is purged, or you are able to ride it out. It is too bad there are no other Immunes to speak with."

A moment passed and I waited for him to expand on his thoughts. It would have all been fine except for one thing.

"Rylee . . ." Eve's voice was groggy, and I jumped to my feet in time to see her slump downward, eyes snapping shut like a virgin's legs on her wedding night. Ah shit.

My blade was in my hand before I finished spinning toward Doran. He stood there, hands in the air. "I could not have her hear what I am about to tell you. For me to even speak it to you will cost me my life if I am caught."

I didn't lower my blade. "You understand why I'm not particularly trusting of you?"

"Rylee, there is so much more going on here than you know. Politics amongst the supernaturals being first and foremost."

"I'm a supernatural, and I don't know anything about any politics," I said, readying myself for an attack from him. I knew from experience the bastard could move like lightening when he wanted to.

"You do not have a group to be a part of, unlike most supernaturals you are a loner. Trackers always are." His eyes lost their glimmer, dulled, and he all but fell back into his chair. "I will not press myself on you.

Your blood still hums through my veins and it makes me want to help. Lucky for you."

I lowered my blade to let the tip trail on the ground. "Will Eve be alright?"

"It was a herb; like catnip for harpies. They crave it and it can put them out in seconds." Now that would be handy to have on hand. Just in case.

"Sit down, Rylee. This will take more than a few minutes."

Reluctantly, I did as he asked, plunking my ass into the over-stuffed patio chair. "Spill it."

"Let us deal with the venom first. I will have to touch the spot where the demon pierced you."

Damn it. "One hand only." I rose up and walked over to him, heart suddenly in my throat. It was no worse than the last time when I'd had to give him blood for information, yet in its own way it was far more intimate.

Doran stood as I drew close and I opened up both jackets and slid my t-shirt down, baring my breast-bone and a healthy view of my black lace bra. The shivering took me immediately.

Lifting one hand, Doran traced the lines of the scar that here, across the Veil, could be seen without us-ing his second sight. The black snowflake shifted and moved as the wind hit it. As if it was real.

"Hoarfrost demon. That's bad, and it confirms what I already thought. It will get worse for you, the cold growing until you are incapacitated," Doran said, his eyes focused on the snowflake as his fingers skimmed the edges of it.

I thought perhaps he would try something, but true to his word, he held off. There was no sensation of him touching me; it was if there was a block between his skin and mine where the snowflake was.

"The demon venom, it is not like anything else. You're lucky you are an Immune, otherwise . . . ."

I nodded and stepped back, straightening my shirt. "Yeah, new ice age and all that jazz."

"Do not be flippant about this, Tracker. It could still happen. Your immunity is protecting you from something that is beyond chaos; it would be world-wide devastation if it came to pass."

That was not expected.

"How do I get it out of me?"

"Heat. Lots and lots of heat. You need to sweat it out while being surrounded by the proper protective spells, and held in the arms of one you trust to keep you safe while vulnerable. It is, to say the least, complicated. And it would require more than one Shaman. Which will be difficult with the other four missing."

I stared at him. No Shaman would ever willingly give up so much information, not even Louisa, and I would count her as one of my few friends. "Faris scares you that badly?"

Everything in the Daywalker tensed, right down to the tips of his spiky hair that seemed to quiver. "If you are not afraid of him, you are a fool. Since he sent you to me, it means he does not want you to have this demon venom coursing through you. He wants you as his own, Rylee. That would not be . . . healthy for you."

The pause in his words, his stance, everything put me on edge. I could feel the energy swirling around, the tension feeding off our fears. "If there's more, tell me. Did you take the other Shamans?"

He shook his head. "No. I had nothing to do with their disappearance."

"Or the fact that Louisa is back and claiming Dox raped her?"

His eyes widened and he pursed his lips. "Louisa would have killed the ogre before he raped her. She is a powerful Shaman."

We stared into each other's eyes, locked in a battle of wills. "Tell me where she is."

"I don't know."

I'd had enough; Ricky was waiting on me, I had no time to waste. Flicking my blade upward, I advanced on him. "One way or another, Doran, you are going to help me. You know more than you are letting you on."

He didn't back away, just let me get closer with my blade aiming for his heart. "I do not know where Louisa and the other Shamans are. Why don't you Track them?"

"Not the point. I think you had something to do with them going missing. Your talk of politics and your fear of the vampire makes me think you're hiding something." Gods, I was starting to sound like O'Shea. What did it matter if I was on the edge of vampire politics? Who the fuck cared who ran their world?

My blade touched his chest, slicing through the material of his shirt. "Talk to me, Doran. You can always say I forced you."

Laughing, Doran batted my blade away; I brought it back to rest over his heart. "Rylee, I cannot tell you anything or my life will be forfeit. As it is, I am walking a fine edge. Find Louisa and the other Shamans, and I will help you purge the demon venom. On two conditions."

Always something.

"What?"

Again, he pushed the blade down. "The first is, I want the demon venom we purge."

It probably wasn't a good idea to let him get his hands on it, but I couldn't see a way around this. "Fine. And what's number two?"

Grinning at me, his green eyes were back to their lively sparkle and he leaned toward me. "A kiss from your lips. No fangs."

I grimaced. "Seriously? You can have that now as a down payment." I moved to close the distance between us, but he raised his hand.

"No, at a time when I choose."

Bloody Shamans were all the same. Even when they said they were helping, they were causing more grief. "Fine. But no funny business."

He put his hand over his heart and the nick I'd given him. "I swear it. Now, go find your Shaman; I will begin to prepare the ceremony to draw out the venom. And one more thing." He tossed me something, a sparkling black jewel on a thin leather band. I caught it with my free hand and the cold rushed out of me in a flash of heat. I stared down at the black gem. Red flames sparkled through it, moving as if were alive, not unlike the snowflake. My fingers clenched the small jewel and I lifted my eyes to Doran.

He smiled. "A fire opal. It won't last more than forty-eight hours, but it will hold the cold at bay for you. Long enough to find Louisa and the others, I think. One thing you should know, wearing the opal will hold the cold at bay, but when it runs out, the cold will have multiplied."

"In other words, don't drop it," I said.

Doran tugged at his lip ring with his right fang, and gave me a nod. Got it, don't drop the fire opal or I was going to be in even worse trouble than now.

I swallowed the thanks on the tip of my tongue, settling for a smile and stepped back from him. Already the heavy buffalo jacket felt too warm.

Making as if he would leave, I tapped him on the shoulder with my blade, and pointed at the sleeping Harpy. "You forgot something."

"Ah, right. The Harpy. How angry will she be when she wakes?"

"She's always pissy when she's been disturbed."

He tossed me a small bag I caught easily. "Put that under her beak, it will rouse her."

I sniffed the contents. "Smelling salts?"

But the daywalker Shaman had already disappeared, leaving it up to me to explain what had happened.

I slid the fire opal on, intensely glad I had it. Holding the bag under Eve's nose, I waited for it to take effect, mulling over what Doran had told me, what he hadn't, and what I could figure out from his almost cryptic words. He'd mentioned vampire politics, but never explained. Maybe that was what he was worried about getting in trouble for? Possibly. Better than all that, the fire opal hanging around my neck rested against the snowflake, holding the venom at bay. This was more than I'd expected when I'd come to Doran. I was going to have to be nicer to the Daywalker next time I saw him.

Eve came around with a start, eyes blinking, beak snapping. "Where is that little bastard? I will rip his head off!" She screeched, wings flapping as she spun in a circle before settling her eyes on me.

"Did you kill him?"

I had to force myself to keep my feet still at the look in her eye. "No. I'm sorry, Eve. He didn't tell me what he was up to until after he'd done it."

She ruffled her feathers. "I do not wish to be here any longer, it stinks." Her eyes darted around though, showing her discomfort.

Climbing up onto her back, I settled in for the ride back to the Landing Pad, gripping her body with my legs. "Okay, let's head back."

She launched into the air with one smooth jump, wingtips brushing the tops of Doran's home. "Will Alex be angry with you for leaving him?"

"It's not Alex I'm worried about." I thought about O'Shea. Damn, he was going to be royally pissed when we got back.

"I think the agent will be the one who will shout at you. He acts as though he has some say in your do-ings."

I started to answer her, but she kept on talking over me.

"It's as if he thinks he is your mate, as if he alone is able to help you. Phaw, my mother told me all men are like that, full of themselves, thinking they are always needed when in fact they aren't."

Ducking my head against the sharp wind, grateful for the fire opal, I chose not to answer.

Dealing with O'Shea was not going to be fun, but really, when had it ever been? *How about when he planted those lips of his on yours?*

Hunching my shoulders, I tried to insulate myself from my own traitorous thoughts. Motherfucking hormones had the better of me as I replayed the scene in the hotel room, the hard lines of his body.

Eve's voice caught me unaware, so deep into my own thoughts as I was. "Are you all right, Rylee?"

"Yeah. I'm fine."

The Harpy banked hard and I clung to her back, shouting over the wind. "Hey, are you trying to drop me?"

She shook her head, clacking her beak. "No, but I think we are being followed."

I twisted around as best I could without letting go, my eyes widening at what I was seeing. Yup, we were being followed, but I had no idea why. Okay, sure, there were a few people who'd like to see me dropped from a hundred feet up, but not people that had the ability to rouse what I was seeing.

With a wingspan that matched Eve's, but with a sleeker, more predatory body, I stared into the unblinking eyes of a giant eagle. It was like a super-sized version of a bald eagle, every detail of it as clear as if it were sitting beside me. Beak opening, it screamed a challenge, the cry wrapping around us. Eve shuddered below me.

"That is not an ordinary eagle."

"No shit! What is it?"

Again she shivered, her wing strokes faltering, and we slowed considerably. That was not what we needed right now. Again, I had to remind myself Eve was a child, and I was supposed to be looking after her.

"As soon as we're out of its territory, it'll bugger off. Just fly!" I hoped I was right about this. I knew birds were territorial, but who the hell knew how big the eagle's territory was?

Her shivering eased, and her wings took up a steadier rhythm.

Maybe I could figure out what the big bird was up to. Reaching out with my Tracking ability, I touched on the emotions of the raptor behind us.

Blood lust filled me, a rage so intense and hot I felt it coil into my bones. Visions of viscera and broken flesh flittered in front of my eyes, the triumphant scream of the eagle filling my mind.

Shit.

As if sensing my intrusion, the eagle screamed, picking up speed.

"Eve—"

"I'm going to drop fast." She called out.

Tucking her wings tight to her body, she dropped like a stone before she'd even finished speaking. My legs whipped out behind me and I fought to keep a hold of the Harpy with my arms, fingers slipping through her feathers like silk. With everything I had, I fought to stay on board, knowing there was no rescue if I fell. The world around us blurred and my eyes watered past the point of being able to see, the sudden plummet jerking my stomach into my throat. My arms cramped from the strain, the G-force slowly pulling me off Eve's back. Damn it, this was not how I saw myself going out. Dropped from a Harpy's back, not exactly how I'd planned to end things.

As suddenly as she'd dropped, Eve leveled out, skimming the desert floor. Flat out on her back, I crawled forward, pulled my legs back around her, and gripped her sides for all I was worth.

A quick search around us—no big-ass eagle to be seen. Letting out a slow breath I tucked my head against Eve's neck. "We're clear."

"No." She tipped her beak up, directing my eyes right above us. "We're not."

9

"**O**h, fuck me," I whispered. The eagle dropped fast and hard, its trajectory more than obvious. We were about to get slammed into the hard desert ground, our bodies crushed by talons and sheer force. There was nothing I could do but count each breath, hoping I would get one more.

Everything slowed, the air around us humming with the beat of two giant sets of wings. I couldn't look away from the eagle, its eyes locked on mine with a hatred so intense I could feel it.

"HANG ON!" Eve screamed, rolling as the eagle reached for us. Gasping, I tightened my body around Eve's. She rolled in the air, my head brushing against the sand, a thump jarred through Eve and into me, my eyes seeing the world upside down for a split second before coming upright once more.

Two strokes of her wings and Eve had us above the desert again. I looked over her shoulder to see the eagle sprawled out on the ground in a tangle of wings.

"What did you do?"

"I locked claws with him, and then used his momentum to fling him around and into the earth." The pride in her voice was obvious, and I couldn't help myself from whooping with excitement. Maybe having a Harpy around wasn't such a bad thing.

"Eve, you're AMAZING!" I pumped one fist into the air.

Letting out a screech of her own, she spiraled on an updraft. Her pride, pure and unadulterated, was written all over her face, eyes bright. "I did good?"

"You did better than good, you rocked his ass!" I never thought I'd be so happy to have a Harpy on my side. I gave her a thumbs up. "Eve, you are going to be one hell of a gal when you grow up."

Her body fluffed up and she took a deep breath. "I learned that from my father, before he left us. I think he would be proud of me today."

Lips pressed together, I fought the emotions surging up in me. I knew what it was to want to be daddy's girl, to have your father proud of you.

"I think you're right, Eve. He would be proud of you." I paused and laid a hand on her back. "I'm proud of you."

The glimmer of a tear shone in her eye as she turned her head away from me. "We're almost back."

Below us the Landing Pad came into view. Circling around the motel once, Eve brought us in slow, landing so softly I barely felt it. Sliding off her back, I turned to see O'Shea striding out of the motel, features twisted with anger. Yes, that was how I needed to deal with him. Balls to the wall, pissed off, and ready to strangle me.

"Adamson! What. Do. You. Think. You're. Doing?" He came to a stop just inches in front of me, our toes nearly touching.

Cocking one hip, placing a hand on it, I shrugged. "Just getting things done. I told you Doran wasn't a guy you should be messing with. I meant it. He knocked Eve out within three minutes of us being there."

O'Shea gave Eve a once over. "Yet, she's fine."

I pushed past him, calling over my shoulder. "Good job, Eve. I'm going to look into a harness, so we can practice once we get home."

She danced on the spot, hopping from one foot to the other, beak clacking. At least she was happy.

Heavy footsteps followed me into the semi darkness of the motel—a hand grabbed my arm, spinning me around. Dark eyes stopped my mouth, the anger in them was expected, but not the concern. Not the worry.

"How can I help you, how can I keep you alive, if you won't let me in? And why aren't you freezing your ass off? Did he actually get the venom out of you?" His words ignited a strange mixture of emotions in me. Damn him.

"I am not your job, I'm not—"

"We're in this together. Whether you like it or not, I think of you as my partner. Which means where you go, I go. No exceptions." His grip loosened on me, and I rubbed my arm. I didn't need him, had never needed him before.

Someone cleared their throat and we both looked up—Dox leaned against the bar. "How was Doran?"

I gave a sharp nod. "Same as last time, pain in the ass daywalker. But he gave me this." I held up the fire opal, and then hung up Dox's long jacket. Heading over to the bar, I poured myself a glass of orange juice. A deep snore rattled from the far side of the room where a hammock had been set up in the corner. Alex lay in it, limbs dangling at strange angles of the edge. No doubt Dox had stuffed him full of food; it was the one surefire way to knock the werewolf out.

"Hitting the heavy stuff already?" Dox teased as I drank the cool liquid down.

"Shut up," I grumbled. He knew I couldn't handle stimulants; my body just wasn't designed for things like high amounts of sugar or small amounts of alcohol.

O'Shea tapped the bar with his fingers as he moved to lean against the bar beside me. "Did you get what you needed?"

I rubbed the back of my neck. "First things first. Dox, why is there a giant eagle flying around?"

The ogre's eyes widened and he stared at me as if I'd just sprouted two heads. "There isn't."

"Yes. There is. It attacked me and Eve on our way back."

"Which," O'Shea decided to point out, "wouldn't have happened if we'd gone together in the SUV."

Lips pursed in a thin line of anger, I fought the urge to shove him. "If we'd gone into its territory, even with a SUV, and it chose to pursue us, we'd be carried off and dropped in some large canyon, SUV and all."

"Whoa, whoa. There are no giant eagles. That sort of stuff is . . ." Dox said , his eyes going distant for a split second. "Unless it is another of the tribal Guardians."

This day was just getting better and better.

"Explain, please, what happened with Louisa," I said, pulling up a barstool.

Dox clasped his overly large hands in front of him. "She showed up at my door looking like death warmed over. I barely recognized her to be honest. Her tribal Guardian was with her." He lifted his eyes to mine, the strain around the edges highlighted by the shadows of the room. "He's a big boy, about my size, but man, he cleaned my clock like he was taking out the trash, like my blows were nothing to him."

I went to his side and touched his arm. "I need to know what we're dealing with."

The ogre slipped one arm over my shoulder. "I've never been in a fight where I knew I was going to lose. The Guardian hit me once, and I knew that no matter what I did, I was done."

Son of a bitch, if Dox was scared, we were in more trouble than I'd thought.

"Do you think it was really Louisa? I mean, could it have been someone in disguise? You said you barely recognized her."

He shrugged. "I don't know. But how would she have called forth a Guardian if it wasn't her?"

Good point. I wracked my brain, but it was O'Shea who asked the smart question.

"Could she have been coerced, forced to do this?"

Both Dox and I just stood there, staring, the idea of someone forcing a Shaman to do anything hard to swallow. And yet . . .

"I never would have thought of it," I said, fingers reaching for my sword handle. In my mind, I preferred the idea of Louisa manipulating us, like pieces

on a chessboard. It was a far uglier idea that someone
else controlled the powerful Shaman.

Dox shook his head. "Me either. Not a Shaman of
her stature. But it might make sense."

It was O'Shea who turned the conversation back to
me. "What did Doran say?"

"I need Louisa and the other Shamans, along with
Doran and a few other details, to get the venom out of
me. Then we're good to go."

"What few other—"

"Venom?"

The two men—and I use that term loosely, considering one of them was an ogre—talked over one
another.

An irritated sigh left me, and I quickly filled Dox in
on the demon, the venom, and the problem with the
cold. Then, for the next fifteen minutes, we went over
the details of Dox's problem. Gods be damned, as if
one issue at a time wasn't enough. Louisa hadn't been
back, and hadn't been seen since her visit to Dox. The
idea that she was being coerced was the only thing that
we could agree on. Because even though she could be
manipulative—the way of all Shamans—I had a hard
time seeing her use that method on Dox. She had
always been quite fond of the ogre, often visiting him
for coffee and to gossip about the local shenanigans.

All of which only made this situation stranger.

Tentatively, while Dox and O'Shea rehashed what
we knew, I closed my eyes and reached out with my
mind to Track Louisa. What I felt though, was, for
lack of a better term, off. It was almost like she was on
the other side of the Veil, but not quite. The energy of

her life force hummed steadily, and the soft brush of her emotions was there, but they were muted. I was pretty sure I could find her, turning to the south facing windows, knowing that was the direction she was in. Okay, but what was this haze over her? It was like a blanket of thick fog that left you knowing there was a person in front of you, but you were unable to see them clearly.

"Something's blocking me from her," I said. "And she isn't on the other side of the Veil. It feels like she's trying to muffle her threads, her life force, as if she doesn't want to be found."

The two guys stopped talking, Dox lifted his eyebrows and O'Shea just watched me. Shifting on my feet, I worried my bottom lip with my teeth. With all that was going on, I was reluctant to make a snap decision, unusual as it was for me.

"Listen, I want to go out to her place, it's in the direction I'm feeling the pull from anyway. Maybe we can find something to help us."

O'Shea laughed. "You mean, like Louisa?"

I smiled over at him. "Yeah, if things are that simple." Which with my life, they rarely were.

Alex snorted in his sleep, barked, and woke himself up with a start. With a grunt, he tried to flip himself out of the hammock, and ended up sprawled on the floor.

"I think we should leave him here," O'Shea said, touching my arm. I watched Alex's sleepy face turn to one of irritation, his amber eyes tracking O'Shea's hand as it trailed down my arm. "Until you do something about this, he's going to be a problem." O'Shea had curved his body around mine, with each breath touching more of me. Alex climbed to all fours, fur standing at attention, a low growl rumbling in his throat.

It was Dox who broke the tension. "You know why he's doing this, don't you?"

I shook my head, and put a hand on O'Shea's chest, creating some distance between us. "I sure as hell wish I did."

"You are his pack leader, Rylee. And I doubt he's ever had any other competition for your affection. Am I right?" Dox flushed, his skin going a light purple shade.

"Fuck, but he's submissive! He shouldn't be challenging anyone." I threw my hands into the air.

Dox knocked his big knuckles on the counter. "But O'Shea isn't a werewolf, so he's more like prey than another predator. Easy pickings when it comes to keeping his pack intact. Even a submissive wolf will fight for their pack leader. Probably just comes and goes with him, doesn't it? One minute he's submissive, the next aggressive?"

I nodded. Dox's lips curled up on one side. "I'd bet a case of beer he's struggling with it. He's a submissive of course, but wants to protect you. It will make him unpredictable at best until there is a definitive laying down of the law."

Gods be damned, I glanced over at the werewolf who continued to stalk towards us, body and hair stiff.

"Alex, knock it off." He froze in mid stride, his hackles slowly going down, and I turned to Dox. "Any other particular tidbits you'd like to share? Like how to get him to stop this?"

"Stop touching the agent."

It was my turn to flush, and then stammer. "It's not me!" Flustered beyond belief, I pointed at Alex. "You stay here with Dox." Next, pointing at O'Shea. "You come with me." Striding for the door, I chose to ignore the deep rumble of Dox's laughter, a soft word, and then O'Shea's laugh from behind me. Men, who the hell needed them? Surely, not me. I looked over my shoulder, caught O'Shea's eyes as he watched me walk ahead of him. That would have been all fine and dandy if he hadn't winked at me. One slow, promise-filled wink from a dark eye that sparked all kinds of naughty thoughts in my head. Damn, I was so screwed.

He enjoyed watching Rylee get flustered, liked to watch her in-control exterior crack. But more than that, he liked knowing he was the one to make her blush, to make her skin hot, and her pupils dilate. Buggered, he was so buggered by this woman it nearly made him forget Agent Valley's threat. Would it matter to him if she wasn't his partner on paper, if he had her in his bed? The thought of her naked and writhing beneath him, her words a whispered plea in his ear, made him forget for a moment how very angry he was with her. How only moments before he'd wanted to strangle the life out of her for scaring him, taking off with the Harpy like that. And the waiting . . . the not knowing if she was coming back.

"Stop dawdling, Agent." She slid into the driver's side with a flick of her auburn hair. Dawdling?

One way or another, O'Shea knew he would get Rylee to trust him. Damned if he knew how, but he would fight for it. If all she would give him was a partnership on the job, then he'd take it. Though, by the returning heat he saw in her eyes, he suspected he wasn't the only one thinking naughty things. That made him smile as he opened the passenger's door and jumped into the SUV.

"What are you so happy about?"

Trust, trust came with honesty. Biting the bullet, he said the first thing that came to mind.

"I was thinking about the hotel room."

It was if all the air got sucked out of the vehicle in one fell swoop. He turned in his seat to see her staring at him, lips parted, tri-colored eyes wide and showing more green and gold than brown.

"You . . ."

He shrugged, pleased by her reaction and trying his best not to show it. "Are we going, or staying?"

Rylee's mouth shut with a click and she turned the vehicle on, backed out a little too fast, spitting gravel out all around them. "We're going."

Seeing as she'd used her wiles on him on their last case to keep him off balance, it seemed only fitting that he reverse the tables on her.

They drove in silence for about ten minutes before he decided to chance a conversation. "What could be blocking you from feeling Louisa properly if she isn't on the other side of the Veil?"

Amusement flitted through him as he saw her sigh of relief at his question.

"I'm not sure. Usually kids are on this side of the Veil, or the other, dead or alive. This fuzzy limbo shit is not something I've run into before." She pushed her back deep into the seat, arms poker straight. "But Ricky is still hanging on. He's still asleep; I think the Ass Hat has him sedated."

O'Shea nodded. "The kid will hang on, the Troll wants you. He'd doesn't give a shit about the kid."

"I know. That's what worries me. Shit on a stick. We have to get to Louisa, and find the other Shamans."

He didn't respond. The thing he'd learned early on as an agent was that there was always another case. There was always someone else who needed you more. In this kind of a job you had to at some point become inured to the fact that you couldn't save them all. It just wasn't possible. Looking at her profile, the tight worry around her eyes, the grim line of her mouth, he knew better than to share that truth.

And maybe she would be one of the lucky ones. Perhaps that was why he made a promise he shouldn't have. "We'll get it done. We'll help Louisa, she'll help you, and we'll save the kid."

She gave him a quick look. "Even I know you're trying to make me feel better. Thanks, but it isn't necessary. I don't need the moral boost. You do the best you can. Some people make it, some people don't. And the Ass Hats of the world get smoked in between."

A grin slipped across his face; he had underestimated her. Yet again, she was proving herself to be the kind of woman he thought didn't exist.

He closed his eyes, leaned his head back in his seat, and did his best to concentrate on the case, flipping it from all angles. The problem was, with his eyes closed, all he could see was a naked Rylee beckoning to him, her sweet lips curving into a smile as she wrapped her arms around him. Which, while more than pleasant, did nothing to help him concentrate.

"Fuck." He grumbled, shifting his ass, wishing he'd worn tighter pants.

"What's got your knickers in a knot?"

He almost told her. Almost.

10

We pulled into Louisa's property, a large south-western style gate arcing over the entrance, complete with the skull of a bull on the crest of it. I rolled down my window, driving slow enough that the crunch of my tires on the dirt was the only noise. There was no hum of energy, no telltale scent of a spell leaking through.

"You think we're going to sneak up on her?"

I wasn't sure if he was being an ass or not, all his mumbling and grumbling on the drive made me wonder if he'd gotten into some of Dox's ogre beer after all.

"No. I want to be able to slam it into reverse in case we set off any booby traps." I smiled sweetly over at him. "You know what a booby trap is, don't you?"

The agent rolled down his window and craned his head out to have a look. "What am I looking for?"

"You ever smell the air right before lightning strikes?" I kept my eyes glued to the road ahead of us, watching for indentations or obvious scuff marks.

He slowly drawled out, "Yeah. Fantastic." And stuck his head back out the window.

Parking in front of the sprawling rancher, I didn't see anything that screamed trouble. Of course, it wasn't like Louisa would be putting a freaking sign out over each potential death spell. It wasn't me I was worried about, but O'Shea was as vulnerable as anyone else to a spell designed to kill. On second thought, with the demon venom coursing through me, my immunity to spells could be diminished. Son of a bitch, I had to get this shit out of me.

Turning the SUV off, I stepped out and did a slow circle. The place felt totally abandoned. Tracking Louisa was easy; I locked onto her almost right away. I turned again, feeling the Shaman's energy spike, and with a pop the clarity was gone and I was dealing with the fuzzy fog.

"What the hell?" I took a step toward the house. She was inside, of that much I was sure, but why the change in clarity?

O'Shea moved with me, pulling a sword off his back. With his long trench coat, it was well hidden, unlike mine. "What is it?"

"Louisa is in the house." I sent out a thread to Track her again. She was at the back of the house, shifting back and forth. I motioned for O'Shea to join me and opened the door.

The interior of the Shaman's house was decorated with classic southwestern decor. Nothing that stood out, but here and there I noted pieces, some far from the norm, different than anything else I'd seen here in the past. The skull of an eagle with cactus spines sticking out of it, a triad of claws, connected by woven sinew that looked like a primeval throwing star, and a stone-carved bowl that, upon closer inspection, held candies. Okay, maybe the candies weren't odd, but the carved bowl was made out of the top of some sort of skull. Nice. I scooped up a candy on my way by, popping it into my mouth, much to O'Shea's surprised intake of air.

"You think that's a good idea?"

I rolled the candy in my mouth, the taste of honey and lemon circling. "I've been here before, the candies are good."

The scuff of a chair on the floor stopped us both, my hands pulling out both of my blades instantly at hearing it. Another scuff and the creak of steps on the floor sent a chill down my spine. I didn't want to surprise the Shaman; her abilities were not to be discounted in any way.

"Louisa, it's me, Rylee. I'm here with my partner, O'Shea. We'd like to talk to you." Funny how easy it was to put him out there to others as my partner.

The footsteps paused and then started up again, this time faster, shifting from a lightweight tread to a heavy thump that resounded through the house.

"Adamson . . ."

"Don't let her touch you." I crouched. "And don't kill her."

There was a moment where everything paused, the air around us stilling, the pulse of my blood slowing, and then the world seemed to explode.

Brown fur, claws, and teeth like daggers, came roaring at us, swiping with frying pan-sized paws. This was the tribal Guardian Louisa had called up. A bear and a big one at that.

I changed my mind. "Shit, kill it!" I swept my blade out, catching the bear across the forearm. I expected a spurt of blood, a misplaced step, something.

The skin split and immediately stitched itself back together. O'Shea drove the point of his sword deep into the bear's side, straight through the heart.

The bear roared, saliva dripping from its lips and teeth, and caught the agent in the hip, sending him flying back the way we'd come, crashing through a table on the way. Again, there was no blood. The bear hunched its back and rose on its back feet, roaring at me, lips pulled back, the scent of death and blood on its breath. Its eyes found me, and I was drawn into them, the silver orbs not of this world. Tribal Guardian, indeed.

A howl echoed from outside and a scrabble of claws on the floor spun me around in time to see Alex launch himself at the bear, muzzle and claws extended.

"Alex, no," I yelled, unable to stop him. Why the hell hadn't he listened to me and stayed with Dox?

The werewolf hit the bear hard, head on, digging his back claws into the bear's underbelly, teeth into his neck. And though the creature should have been eviscerated, it continued to come at us. With an almost casual fling of its claw-tipped paw, it pulled the wolf off and threw him at the window. Glass shattered all over the floor, and Alex disappeared. This had to stop. We couldn't fight this one and survive. Taking a step back, I tried to slow my heart, stop the adrenaline pumping through me.

With the calmest voice I could manage, I spoke to the bear. "We mean no harm." This after I yelled to kill it, ha! "I'm here to help Louisa." I lowered the tips of my blades, fighting my instincts, which were to try and take the creature's head. But if Louisa had called it up, I doubted even a decapitation would stop the bear.

The bear dropped back to all fours, still staring at me. Swallowing hard, I held my ground. "You are here to protect Louisa; I'm here to do the same."

Sounds of movement from behind me told me O'Shea wasn't out cold, and the groan from outside told me Alex was moving, if slower than before. The bear hadn't moved forward, just watched. I had no idea if the thing could understand me or not, but I was banking on it.

"Tell Louisa we're here. We'll wait for her."

The bear let out a low rumble, swiping at the floor with its paw and leaving a trail of gouge marks in the ground, a reminder of what it could do to us. Then, slowly, it backed out of the room, disappearing into the back of the house. Silence fell, as if the bear had never been.

I ran to where O'Shea was just now sitting up, a hand over his hip. Three claws had caught him, tearing through skin down to the bone.

"You're lucky this wasn't your belly," I said, poking at the wounds. They needed to be stitched, but they weren't life-threatening. I took a look over the rest of him; lots of scrapes and he'd likely be bruised, but he'd live. Alex stumbled in from outside, his face cut up and dripping blood. Limping over to us, head hung low, he whimpered, shaking his head several times, drool flinging around the room. "I try help."

I beckoned him closer and he laid down beside O'Shea, head on the agent's thigh.

"Yeah, I know." I stroked the wolf's head, smoothing out the wounds as they sealed themselves up. A little like the Guardian, only I knew that in Alex there was blood and a beating heart that could be stopped.

"Did you talk to that thing?" O'Shea asked while I poked at Alex, checking him over too.

Shrugging, I nodded. "You never know until you try. I'm pretty sure it is Louisa's Guardian, the one that roughed up Dox. He never told us it was a bear though."

A deep voice rumbled from behind us and I spun, lifting a blade.

"That is because I can be both man and beast, one of those destined to protect his people."

Tall, heavily muscled, with long black hair pulled back over one ear, the man standing before us looked as though he'd stepped through time. Sun-darkened skin and deer hide pants were his only article of clothing besides a large bearskin, head and everything, that hung around his shoulders. His bare feet—no pun intended—slapped the floors lightly.

"Louisa is waiting for you on the back porch."

I rose, O'Shea following stiffly.

The Guardian stepped forward, silver eyes glaring. "Only you, Tracker. Not the human. And not the wolf."

O'Shea glared back, the level of testosterone rising rapidly. Alex lifted his head, snarling up at the Guardian, white teeth flashing, saliva dripping from his lips. Fabulous.

"I'll be fine, O'Shea. Just wait for me. Alex, you stay with O'Shea. Keep him safe." Alex frowned, but nodded slowly, then shook his head, spittle flying everywhere.

"Doody."

O'Shea's gaze shifted from the Guardian to me, the glare not lessening. "I don't trust him."

"There isn't a choice. Besides, I think he could have snapped us like twigs if he'd wanted to." I lifted an eyebrow at the Guardian who gave me a small nod of acknowledgment. Yup, good to know when you could be wiped out and by whom. I was no superwoman, no secret agent. There would always be creatures out there that could out muscle me. And it was important to remember that truth.

Leaving a muttering O'Shea and a grumbling Alex behind, I skirted past the Guardian. The scent of musk and damp growing things caught me unawares, and I paused for a split second, breathing it in. For a moment it felt like I was deep in a forest, the heavy canopy dripping rain, the crush of greenery surrounding me, the trickle of a stream close by. I shook my head, dispelling the image as the Guardian glanced down at me with a frown. I picked up my pace. Whatever I was picking up from him was not necessary, but I would admit, it piqued my curiosity about the Guardians in general.

I strode through the back room and pushed the porch screen door open, letting it bang behind me. To my right, Louisa, or what was left of her, sat propped up by cushions, her body emaciated to the point where her clavicle and chest bones pressed against her skin. Her once luxurious black hair that brushed the ground when she walked was gone, replaced by a sparse scattering of gray that didn't even reach her shoulder. I'd always put Louisa in her mid- to late thirties, the prime of her life, but now she looked as though she'd aged sixty years since I'd seen her last. The only thing identifying her to me was her eyes, silvery white, identical to the Guardian.

"Oh my God," I whispered, horrified at what could have done this to her.

"Not so pretty now, am I?" She started to laugh, but ended up coughing, blood flecking the white handkerchief she pressed to her lips.

Standing in front of her, I couldn't help but stare, didn't know where to start. To be this far gone, to have so much stripped from her, it was an impossible thought.

"Tell Dox I am so sorry for accusing him. But I needed to get your attention."

My eyes widened at her apology, but I kept my mouth shut and waited for her to finish.

She tipped her head to one side, her eyes flicking away from mine, her voice softening, a slight tremor in it. "I am being watched, by a darkness I cannot shake."

My thoughts went to Faris immediately. Was it him? She went on.

"I was afraid to reach out to you. It is why I thought it best to look as though we were at odds. Whatever is watching me is hungry for power, for blood, for control."

"That why you muffled your threads?"

Nodding, her eyes darted up to mine. "I hoped he would lose interest if he could no longer feel my life force as strong as before."

I licked my lips. "Is he still watching you?"

Her eyes sharpened. "How do you know it is a he?"

"Lucky guess."

That gaze never left my face, and it took everything I had not to squirm. Finally, she answered. "No, who-ever he is, he has removed his presence. Do you know of whom I speak?"

I rolled my shoulders. "Yeah, if it's the same one, I know who it is. A vampire named Faris."

Louisa gripped the edge of her seat, breathing out the word, "Vampire."

The air around us stilled, and then she shook it off. "Enough, he is gone and there is naught I can do for it now. I need your help, Rylee. Desperately."

Rocking back on my heels, I stepped back from her, already knowing what she would ask and knowing that I would do it. "Tell me."

"I would ask a trade. Free my sister Shamans. Stop this" —she waved skeletal hand at her body— "from happening to them. And I will owe you a favor."

"A big ass favor," I said. "Not some round about, 'I gave you iced tea when you came to visit' piece of shit Shaman garbage."

She sucked in a large breath, eyes going wide. I'd never spoken to her that way before. Maybe it was the demon venom.

Nope, I was just pissed off.

"You beat the hell out of Dox, manipulated me into coming down here to rescue your friends, yet every time I needed your help, I had to pay for it. Usually through the fucking nose! Why should I help you?"

Tears glinted in her eyes, but her mouth was a hard line. "Do you not need us to help purge the venom? Would that not be a good enough trade of gifts?"

How the hell had she known? The Shaman spoke again, perhaps seeing the question in my eyes; more likely she just knew me well enough by now.

"I can see it in you, Rylee, the venom flows sluggish in your body, kept at bay by your immunity and the fire opal. But still it flows, seeking an outlet to another person, one it would devour, one it would use to bring about the destruction of the world. It is like a killing charm lying across you, a burden no other could take. If the wolf had been the recipient, even now we'd be facing legions of the undead and demons that our minds could not comprehend. If the child had been the one to take the blow, she would even now be opening portals across the deep levels of the Veil, bringing destruction and chaos to reign on Earth as it has never before done. But you"—she reached out, brushing my hand with her fingers—"you have it in you to contain all that evil with barely a dip in your ability to exist."

"Why are you telling me this?"

"Because I do not think this will be the last time you will have to carry a burden that no other can."

Her words struck me to the core. I did not want to do this again, and I wasn't even at the end of this round.

"My sisters are waiting on you, Rylee. And is there not a child also waiting on you, left behind in the north?"

I closed my eyes, the weight of responsibility to so many as heavy as it got. Shit. Opening my eyes, I pushed it all down. I had a job to do, and I couldn't do it cowering in the fucking corner.

"Where are they, your sisters?"

Louisa shifted in her seat, a grimace twisting her face. "I do not know. I escaped, but only because the creature who held us thought me dead, throwing my body out with the refuse. Hallucinating, delusional with fever, I made my way home on foot, but I have no idea how far I came."

Tapping a sword tip against my boot, I asked, "Do you have something of theirs, something personal I can use to Track them?"

She shook her head. "No, we keep nothing like that of each other's, the temptation to set magic upon each other in the past was too great."

Fabulous. A thought circled around my head, one I considered a distinct possibility. "Which direction did you come from?"

Pointing to the back of the property, she said softly, "The north. Through the mountain pass."

What other choice did I have? I stared in that direction, wishing to hell now that I'd at some point visited one of the other Shamans. Shortsighted—it wasn't something I'd make the mistake of again.

"Rylee, there is something you need to know. The creature who took us, she drained my powers, that is why my Guardian arose. It is why the giant eagle now searches the skies. As a Shaman's powers are drained, their Guardian rises to protect them."

"What is it," I asked, "The creature who took you?"

Louisa's head dropped. "I am not certain. She looked human." We both knew no human could manage this sort of damage on a Shaman.

"Okay." I turned to leave. Her voice called me back.

"You do not understand, Rylee. You need at least four Shamans to draw the venom out of you. If the creature takes another one of my sisters, you will be set to carry this demon with you. But if you kill the creature, our powers will be released back to us."

I looked over my shoulder and gave her a tight smile, my heart racing at the thought of not being able to bring Ricky home. "I guess I'd better get moving then."

Striding through the house, I nodded at the Guardian, one supernatural to another. Grabbing Alex's collar, I gave him a tug. "Come on, boys."

O'Shea followed, limping slightly, blood dripping down his right leg, a big wet spot where Alex had laid his head. Those pants were done for. "Where are we headed?"

"You are headed back to Dox, to get stitched up. Alex and I are going to track Louisa's back trail."

Alex hopped on his back legs. "Alex wins."

"Sit," I snapped, pointing to the ground. Alex slammed his butt into the dirt so hard a puff of dust billowed up around him.

Big amber eyes stared up at me and he whispered, his lips barely moving over his teeth. "Alex wins."

I swore that the male species would be the death of me. "No, you . . . just sit there."

Moving over to O'Shea, I tried to hustle him into the SUV. "I'm not going."

"You can't come with me. You need to get stitches and you can barely walk." I poked him in his hip, making him crumple almost to the ground to prove my point.

Pulling himself back up, he countered. "I'm damn well not leaving you on your own again. You don't know what you're going after . . . ."

I was already shaking my head. "Rarely do I know what I'm going after. It's called flying by the seat of your pants for a reason. It's how I work."

It was hard for me to turn my back on him, to walk away. Because I was starting to rely on having him with me. If nothing else, I knew I wasn't alone. Alex butted his head into my hand, his wounds already healed up, as if they had never been.

"Rylee."

I didn't look back, couldn't. O'Shea's voice had softened. "I can't watch you go off on your own, not again."

I took a deep breath.

"Then close your eyes."

11

He slammed the heels of his hands onto the steering wheel, fury keeping him from feeling the gouges in his leg. *Damn her!* When he'd gone to follow her, that bear Guardian bastard had stepped out on the porch; its freaky silver eyes making him feel every inch the human he was. No words were needed; O'Shea knew the Guardian would never let him pass.

Rylee had walked away, Alex at her heels, happy as a fucking lark. And here he was, so pissed off he could barely see straight.

The Landing Pad came into view in a surprisingly short time. Of course, it didn't hurt that he'd had his foot almost hammered to the pedal the entire way.

Limping his way into the front of the motel, he started hollering for Dox.

The ogre came bounding out from deeper in the building, his eyes widening. "Where is she?"

"She bloody well took off without me again." Of course, he wasn't going to admit there had been no way he could get past the Guardian to go after her. Not to mention his hip being flayed open like a steak.

"Shit. Well, let's get you stitched up so you don't bleed all over the desert looking for her."

"I should just leave her on her own." He grumped, turning so Dox could get a better look at the gouges.

"Louisa's Guardian do this?"

"Yes." He hissed out as the ogre poked at the torn flesh.

"Could be worse. There's lots of blood, and your pants are done for, but it could be worse."

"That's what she said."

Dox pointed him to a table and O'Shea hiked himself up on it, feet propped up by a chair.

The ogre made swift work of the stitches.

"You aren't going to leave her on her own, are you?" Dox lifted his head, pausing in his stitching to ask the question.

"No. I'm not."

"Good. She deserves someone who won't give up when she pushes them away. She does it because she wants to protect you."

He knew, in his gut, she did it because she cared, but hearing it from Dox made it more real.

"She's so damn stubborn." He yelped, his eyes snapping wide, as Dox hit a particularly tender spot.

Laughing, the ogre nodded. "That too. Though I suspect you might match her in that department."

Grunting, he closed his eyes again.

"You need to tell her how you feel, man. She doesn't play games. If she's holding back, there's a reason."

Love life advice from an ogre? "And you would know this how?"

The needle snagged on a piece of skin and he sucked in a sharp breath, almost missing Dox's answer.

"Because she's honest to the core. Foul mouthed, stubborn, at times downright vicious when it comes to protecting those she cares about. But always, she's honest. I don't know that she's got it in her to lie to you. Pin her down, tell her how you feel, and I bet" —Dox tied off the last stitch— "she'll open up."

The idea of pinning her down certainly had its merits. But before he could do that, he had to find her. Again.

"Thanks for the advice." He scrubbed a hand through his hair. "I think."

"Anytime. Want a beer to chase the ache away?"

O'Shea lifted an eyebrow, remembering all too well the hangover from the last beer he'd had at the Landing Pad.

"Thanks, I think I'll pass."

Dox laughed and moved out of the way, giving O'Shea room to get off the table. He stood, wincing when he tried to bear weight on his wounded leg. How the hell was he going to go after her? Sure, he could drive to Louisa's again, but then he'd have to get past the Guardian, which wasn't going to happen. Then there was the terrain, all on foot, with a messed up leg.

A flutter of movement from the courtyard through the window caught his attention, and he turned to Dox, a question in his eyes.

Dox smiled. "Man, it's your life. But it probably would be the best way to catch up with her."

With a ruthful grin, O'Shea limped out into the bright sunlight; that it was, on both counts.

Alex and I kept a steady pace, jogging as he scented the ground, following Louisa's scent backwards to wherever she'd been held.

In theory, it was sound, but there were spots where we lost her trail either from the shifting sand, the time, or the wind, and apparently there had been a rain shower at some point. That was according to Alex, so I didn't wholly believe it was the issue.

The biggest problem I was dealing with was Alex. Even now, sniffing along, he started to veer to one side, tail wagging as he picked up a scent that interested him, taking him from the task at hand.

"Alex, Louisa, not the fucking rabbits," I said, slowing to wait on him.

With a doggy grin of shame, he shrugged. "Fucking rabbits smell good."

I did not want to know that. "You can come back here and smell all you want later, but right now, I need you to find Louisa."

He pointed back the way we'd come, head cocked. "Isa back."

Oh crap. "No, I want you to find her, that way." I pointed in the opposite direction. "Where she was before."

"Gotcha!" And he was off again, following her scent late into the day. We stopped for dinner, sharing one of the 'fucking rabbits' over the fire. I wasn't really hungry, and I was exhausted past the point of being able to sleep, laying there, feeling like I wasn't doing enough. Ricky was waiting on me, and with the three Shamans left, no one else even had a clue where the hell they were. My fire opal was already half used up, which stressed me out. From what Doran said, once I lost it, I would be hammered by the cold. Louisa had been stripped of her powers, but even when I questioned her, she would refer to her captor only as a 'creature.' I had no idea what we were walking into, not even a whisper of a clue. A small part of me wished Milly was here, but then I pushed that away. She wasn't the friend she'd used to be; something had changed in her, taken her away, even if she was back with us in the physical sense.

Then there was O'Shea. I'd hurt him by leaving him behind. But if he died because of me, I wasn't sure I could deal with that. Not again. It was one thing to lose people you knew, but didn't really love, but to lose someone you loved was . . . my thoughts stuttered as I realized what I was thinking.

I was falling in love with the agent.

Everything in me went still, the truth of my own emotions shocking me to the core. Shit, I really didn't like this; it was not in my plan. But, I'd never shied away from the truth before, not even when it hurt me. It just sucked so badly that the first man I felt these emotions for was sleeping with my best friend.

He's not sleeping with her right now. The traitorous side of me spoke up, egging me on to a possibility I refused to consider. It didn't matter that she—Milly—wasn't here. I had my standards, and I would hold to them kicking and screaming if necessary. Which meant no stealing your best friend's man, even if she kinda stole him first. Damn it, I wasn't going to sleep anyway; might as well make something happen.

"Alex." I stood. "Let's get going."

The werewolf got up, stretching with his paws jammed into his lower back, almost like a man. "Yuppy doody," he grunted. "Going."

Dropping his nose to the ground, he started following Louisa's fading scent as I kicked dirt over the small fire we'd started.

The silver glints of Alex's fur were all I had to follow as he followed his nose. I checked my weapons as we walked. Two swords, four daggers, the whip, and a set of cuffs I'd snatched from the SUV. They would come in handy—that is, if Louisa's captor had hands small enough to fit in the cuffs. All the spells I'd left in the SUV, unable to pack them with me without the chance of breaking them on myself. No need to knock my own ass to the ground; there were plenty enough other people willing to do that for me.

We were jogging, our footsteps silent in the almost pitch black night. The moon was dark, and my eyes struggled to keep Alex in sight. Just the flicker of movement paired with the silver tips of his fur kept me on the right track.

As we ran, the terrain slowly shifted from open desert to paved roads and family homes. This was where it was going to get tough.

Alex stopped, sniffing the air and the ground, and then slowly spun a circle. "Hard to smell."

I waited, knowing there was nothing I could do to help. "You can do it, Alex, you can find her."

His ears perked up and his tail wagged with the praise. Jamming his nose onto the cement, he took an exaggerated breath, stilling as he picked something up. "This a way." He took off at a gallop, and I was hard pressed to keep up with him.

We ran down the silent street, our footsteps and breathing the only thing I could hear. At the first stop sign, Alex plunged his nose onto the ground again, lifted his head and howled a long piercing note as he bolted off to the left.

"Alex, no howling," I yelped as lights in the neighbourhood started to flick on, dogs going ape shit and howling along with him. Damn it, the last thing we needed were 'concerned citizens' asking us questions. I turned on the speed, not seeing that Alex had stopped. I slammed into him, tackling him to the ground to try and soften my own impact. Of course, he thought the whole scene was great fun.

"Wrestling!" He grabbed me in a bear hug, pinning my arms to my side.

"No, no wrestling. It was an accident," I grunted out, squirming my way out of his reach. His head drooped.

Getting to my feet, I knocked the dirt off my knees. "Okay, pick up Louisa's scent again."

He let out sigh. "No fun." But did as I asked.

Over the next four hours, we wove our way in and out of subdivisions, and I began to see the major downside to my plan. Louisa had been hiding, and even in her altered state of incoherency, she'd had enough self-preservation to keep herself tucked away from prying eyes.

There was no straight line, and as dawn began to clear the sky, highlighting it pink and orange, I finally called a halt. Both of us were exhausted, but I didn't want to go back to the Landing Pad. There was no way I'd convince O'Shea to stay behind a second time.

Worse, Alex had lost her scent. Weaving back and forth, we traced our steps back to the last place he could pinpoint her. Then, there was nothing, like she had never even been here.

Fatigue clawed at me. We needed a place to crash, if just for a few hours; then I could figure out what we were going to do. Putting my back against an older adobe style home, I worked my way over to the closest window and peeked in, scanning the darkened house. Built into the side of a cliff, it was painted a dark slate to blend into the surrounding area. Might work, if no one was home.

A car engine revved up and the lower level of the house came alive, the garage door opening, and a sleek sports car backing out and taking off. Before the garage door slid shut, I ducked inside, Alex right with me.

The interior of the house was warm, the lights were all out, and it seemed empty. "You hear anyone?"

Cocking his head to one side, Alex listened for a moment and then shook his head. "Nope."

Perfect.

Working our way through the house, I checked all the rooms, eight in total, to make sure we were indeed alone. With no alarm system, we had a perfect place to sleep for a few hours.

Picking the bedroom with the balcony as an escape route if we needed to leave quickly, I closed the door behind us. Leaving my weapons and clothes on, I lay down on the padded mattress and fell asleep within moments, Alex lying across my legs.

You know the saying, 'No rest for the wicked?' Yeah, looked like it was going to apply to me.

The dream hit me hard, Faris standing there, smiling at me like a cat who'd just got into the freaking catnip.

"Hello, Rylee. You are such a pleasant diversion."

I felt for my weapons, feeling nothing at my sides. "Fuck you and let me sleep."

"Tut, tut. Such language on a young lady like yourself." His eyes glinted and he stepped closer, blue eyes shining like jewels, his hands snaking around me faster than I could react. "I like it."

I jerked away from him, slamming my fist up where his chin had been only to find empty air. Faris was standing to one side of me, smiling as if he had all the time in the world. Being a vampire, that wasn't entirely untrue.

"What do you want?" I'd asked it before, but the fucker didn't seem inclined to tell me the truth.

"I want your trust. I want you to come and work for me."

I was shaking my head before he finished the first sentence. "Nope. Something else? 'Cause if not, I've got things to do, people to see, asses to kick."

Laughing, he strolled in a circle around me. "Doran told you something, something that sparked your interest. Ask me the question, I wish to prove you can trust me."

In the back of my mind I was trying to wake up, thinking if I could just wake up then I could . . . what, never go back to sleep again? No, but at least right now I would be away from him.

"Okay, tell me about vampire politics."

He blinked as if I'd asked him an unexpected question. "That is not something I can share with you. Though I suspect you will find out more than you ever wanted to know when it comes to vampires soon enough."

"Then why the fu . . . heck are you here? What possible reason have you got for disrupting my sleep?" Damn, if he liked a potty mouth, the last thing I wanted to do was swear in front of him.

Faris folded his arms and bowed his head almost as if he were praying. "You don't seem to understand the stakes." He chuckled at some joke I obviously wasn't getting. "You will belong to me, one way or another."

He lunged at me and I reacted, flipping into a backward handspring, catching him in the jaw with my boot. With a roar, he came at me, blood dripping from his lips, fangs lowering. It was like fighting with the wind; I couldn't pin him down, his speed was nothing I had ever experienced before.

Despite my best efforts, it took him less than a minute to have me pinned below him. Bucking and writhing, I attempted to throw him off me, but his bloody grin only grew wider. "We can help each other, Rylee. You stand with me, when the time comes, and I'll give you anything you want."

Glaring up at him, fighting the panic that was rising, I didn't dare say anything.

"Now tell me, there's nothing you want?"

"Nothing you can give me."

His voice lowered to a whisper. "What about . . . Berget?"

"She's dead, long ago."

"Then why can't you Track her, isn't that what you do?" The condescension in his voice set me to fighting again, but he held me easily, whispering into my ear. "I know you've seen her, what if I could give her to you, whole, the child she once was?"

I closed my eyes, tremors wracking me. "No, you're a liar." But even to me my voice sounded weak.

His words, though whispered, were made all the more powerful by the fact that there was so much I would give to have what he offered. "I would give you the world, if you would stand with me, Tracker. Everything you want, your sweet little sister, your wolf, I would even let you keep your FBI agent, if you like. I don't mind sharing."

Faris eased off my body, but I lay there on the ground, eyes squinted shut.

"What is your answer, Tracker, Rylee? Will you take my offer? I will not make it again. Your sister for your loyalty to me. A simple oath."

Gods forgive me for what I was about to do, I loved her too much to deny his words, and there was only one answer I could give him.

"Go to hell, you nasty motherfucker."

12

Rage twisted the vampire's features and he dove at me. Claws dug into my side as the vampire's teeth grazed my face, and I jerked awake to find Alex whimpering beside me.

"Someone comes."

Mouth dry, pulse hammering, I rolled from the bed and dry heaved. Shaking hard, I fought to get myself under control.

"Who is it?"

"Bird."

Bird? "Eve?"

Alex shook his head, letting out a low whimper.

Who else but Eve . . . my mind was slow to grasp the threads.

Bird, Eagle Guardian. Shit! That was the last thing we needed. "Come on, we gotta go," I said, forcing the sleep from my limbs, opening the balcony door, then pushing a rusted iron patio chair under the knob. It might buy us a few minutes if we were lucky.

The balcony was only about ten feet up, not too far, and Alex leapt over the railing, landing lightly below. "Catch Rylee," he yelped, holding out his arms, standing awkwardly on his back feet.

"Get out of the way." I waved him off, settled for shimmying down until I could hang from the bottom of the balcony, and then let go. The drop was negligible, but still, Alex grabbed me mid-air.

"Gotcha!"

"Yes, great. We've got to go."

A human scream echoed out above us, twisting and changing until it became the scream of hunting eagle. The glass door shattered as the Guardian burst through, form shifting from man to eagle as he threw himself into open air.

"Find her," I yelled, pushing Alex ahead of me. We had to get back on Louisa's trail; if we couldn't find it, we were screwed.

Arms and legs pumping, I followed Alex, keeping my eyes partially on him, partially on the bright blue sky above. Glimpses of wings teased at the peripheral of my vision. Alex stopped near a slim trail between two homes and I crouched beside him.

"No Louisa. Smell is gone." He pointed to the ground and, though I saw nothing, I trusted him. Gods be damned, we were going to have to backtrack again. That, or her scent was just too old. I didn't want to think about that possibility. If we couldn't find her soon, I was afraid we would be too late for everyone. Louisa, Ricky, and me and my demon venom.

"Let's go back, pick up the last spot you found the trail," I said, but we hadn't taken two steps before a shadow passed over the sun.

The whoosh of wings, and the air around us kicked up dust. Spinning, the giant Eagle shifted into his man form, a formidable opponent in either case.

He spoke low and angry, his words a slew of non-sense to my ears, the Navajo language, if I was hearing it right. I was able to pick out a few words I'd heard Louisa use. Angry, death words. This was a bad spot, one I was pretty sure we were stuck in. Now, I regretted leaving Eve and O'Shea behind. Too little, too late.

We backed away from the Guardian and, though I knew it was useless, I tried to appease him. Hands out, I said, "We're here to help, not hurt. Louisa, Crystal . . ." buggered if I could remember all the Shaman's names. His eyes narrowed as I stopped listing them off. We couldn't keep running and just hope we would out maneuver the Guardian. I was going to have to rely on my ability to talk to people, convince him we meant no harm.

In other words, we were in deep shit.

Whether it was the moon that rode him, or his affection for me, I have no idea, but Alex took that moment to be brave. Scrabbling around from behind me, he stood in front, hackles raised, hair standing on end. "No hurt Ryleeeeeee!" He howled, teeth gnashing.

The Eagle man stood, staring first at the werewolf, then up at me, then back to the wolf. He was tall, six foot, at least, with nearly black eyes, but a shock of white hair, the same as the eagle he embodied. Leaner than the bear Guardian, every muscle he had was obvious as he took his time looking us over, assessing us. I had the feeling we came up short in his evaluation, as his eyes narrowed and he gave a snort of derision.

I fingered my blades, knowing they would do no good. I wouldn't fight him unless my hand was forced.

I took a breath, adrenaline flooding me, my muscles bunching to sprint away from danger. But the Guardian surprised me.

"Guardian Wolf." He gestured long fingers at Alex, and then his posture relaxed, eyes softening. Maybe we weren't so out of luck.

"Yes. We're here to help the Shamans. To find and free them."

His long white hair shifted in the breeze, and he held his hand out to me. "Eagle will take you there."

"You know where they are held?" Damn, this was better and better.

Eagle nodded. "Come. You free them and I will spare you."

Trust was not something that came easy to me, yet like a war chief of old, I thought the Guardian would honour his word. Dropping one hand on Alex's head, I stroked him behind the ears. "I can't leave my wolf."

"I will carry him."

What other choice did I have? I could try and fight our way out, but since I'd already decided Eagle was worth trusting, it seemed silly to even consider fighting. Still, I wasn't about to actually let him carry us. That was just asking for trouble.

A hot wind snapped down the alley and Eagle shifted his form, smoothly, with barely a ruffle of his feathers.

"We will follow on foot. You lead."

Eagle bobbed his head once and sprung from the ground, straight up. Stepping from the alleyway, I wondered for not the first time at the blindness of the humans around us. A car drove past us, and there was a woman across the street puttering in her flower beds.

Not to say it wasn't better this way; I had no desire to try and explain the giant eagle floating on the currents above us. But I did wonder at what they saw. Maybe just a regular, everyday eagle floating on the breeze?

Breaking into a jog, I followed the path of the eagle, Alex keeping up with me with no problem. Within a short time, we were jogging down a dirt track leading out of the bunch of family homes. Another two miles and the outskirts of the town blurred behind us. Ahead, there was nothing, just expanse of desert, the Guardian filling the sky above us.

I had a feeling we were going to be on the move for a long while.

I was right.

O'Shea clung to Eve's back, sweat dripping down the sides of his face even in the cold air high above the ground. He had to do something to take his mind off the height, and even his anger at Rylee leaving him behind, again, didn't help.

"Eve, how is it that you aren't seen by humans?"

The Harpy tipped her head back to glance at him. "They do not see what their hearts have forgotten. I am a legend, as are the unicorns and many other creatures. Legends are no longer real to humans."

"But you'd show up on radar, wouldn't you?"

"You recall that technology does not work around the supernatural? The rays of your 'radar' are the same. They pass over us as if we are ghosts. That is why, when a human does see us, truly sees us, and takes a pictures, even one close up, it will develop into nothing but shadows and indistinct shapes. The world has moved on and forgotten us. And in that darkness, we are safe from the humans."

O'Shea was silent, the Harpy's words deep and thoughtful for one so young. And somewhat disturbing. He wondered if he ever would have known about the supernatural if Rylee hadn't been the one he'd chased for ten years. And why would the supernaturals need to be safe from the humans? What threat could a human pose to a Harpy, or any of the other supernaturals, for that matter?

"Agent. I think we are getting close to them."

They'd been flying for several hours, their second day on the hunt for Rylee and Alex. He knew the time Doran had bought her with the fire opal was almost up. He and Eve had to find Rylee. As in now.

Yesterday, O'Shea had driven around in the SUV, stopping every hour to meet up with Eve. It had taken some serious convincing on Eve's part to get him on her back. He still wasn't sure it was the right choice, but he had no other option for finding Rylee.

"How do you know?" The wind snatched the words from his lips, though she heard him anyway.

"Eagle."

He looked ahead, and in the far distance he could see a shape, though how Eve could know it was an eagle was beyond him.

"Can't be an eagle; it's too big."

"Trust me, it's an eagle. The one who attacked Rylee and me."

Ice formed around his spine. "Shit, then it's probably tracking them too."

"My exact thoughts." She said no more, but her wings picked up their crescendo, flying them across the desert.

O'Shea hung onto her, remembering all too clearly the wound the bear had inflicted on him. As he'd made to leave the Landing Pad, Dox made a half-hearted attempt to stop him.

"It's what Rylee would expect of me. You know, point out that you're hurt." The ogre had said, a grin splitting his face.

His grin faded when O'Shea had shown him the wound. A scant few hours after he'd been stitched up smooth, thin lines of scar tissue made the stitches unnecessary, and set O'Shea's heart to thumping.

Dox had consoled him. "Likely healed so fast 'cause it was a Guardian. Once they decide you're a friend, they can heal up wounds they've caused."

But O'Shea wasn't so sure.

Pushing the possibilities out of his head, he focussed on the image of an eagle slowly growing larger. Indeed, it was glancing downward to a pair of running figures and seemed unaware they were sweeping up behind him. He had no doubt the eagle was after Rylee and Alex. Eve and he were just in time to pull Rylee's ass out of the fire. A tight smile crept across his face.

"Go high, Eve. Let's hammer him from above."

She chuckled, her head bobbing. "Yes, let's give him a taste of his own medicine."

I paused for a breath, my mouth dry and grit-filled, heart pumping hard. The scent of sage grass was heavy in the air, about the only good thing I could say about the run. If it had been Eve with us, I would have taken the ride by now, but from what I gathered Eagle would not have been letting us ride, so much as gripping us with his talons. Nope, I'd rather run. The problem was how long it was taking. The fire opal was warm against my chest, but I knew I didn't have much longer before my forty-eight hours were up. We had to find the Shamans. Like now.

"How much farther?" I shouted up to our guide. Eagle tossed his head once. Gods, I hoped that meant only one more mile; I couldn't keep this pace up much longer. My legs and arms felt leaden, exhaustion creeping through them with each step I took. Alex, on the other hand, looked as fresh as a daisy. Bloody werewolf.

Grinning around a lolling tongue, he kept pace with me easily, and looked as though he could do another fifty miles no problem. I was almost ready to take Eagle up on his offer of a ride when a familiar screech filled the air. High above Eagle, Eve plummeted, claws outstretched, an all too familiar rider on her back. Damn O'Shea. He just couldn't sit tight and wait for me.

"No, Eve! Stop," I shouted, waving my arms, but the Harpy was in a free fall plummet, her target the one being who could lead us to the Shamans. There was nothing I could do but watch as the two giant birds slammed into one another, their shrieks piercing my ears. Eve's claws burrowed into Eagle's back, clamping one wing down, leaving the other to beat uselessly, spinning them into a tight spiral toward the ground. Eve screamed for all she was worth, and Eagle screamed right back as he struggled to escape her grip. Forty feet up, Eagle twisted hard to one side, throwing Eve off balance and unseating O'Shea who flipped off her back. For a brief second, I fought what I was seeing. O'Shea's body hung, seemingly suspended in the air as the two giant birds struggled all the way down to the ground. And then he fell, hard, hitting the ground with a meaty thump. My guts twisted, knowing there was nothing I could do to save him.

I sprinted toward where O'Shea was crumpled; at least he hadn't hit any rocks, but that high up, I wasn't sure, rocks or not, that he would be alive when I reached him.

All but falling, I put a hand to his face, scratches from the thorny underbrush beside him already welling up with blood.

"O'Shea?"

He groaned and rolled to his side. "Damn it. You better get a riding harness for that bird of yours."

Shocked, I didn't stop to think, just wrapped my arms around him and helped him to sit up. His arms circled back around me, and for just a moment I let myself enjoy the moment. "I thought—"

"Yeah, me too." He pulled back a little, three scratches running down the side of his face, blood dripping, but to me, he had never looked so good. A light seemed to flash in his eyes and he pulled me tight against him, clamping his lips over mine. I clung to his shoulders, forgetting the world around us, tears springing up in my eyes. He could have died, and I never would have been able to see him again, not even on the other side of the Veil where ghosts walk. No human ghosts went to the other side of the Veil; it wasn't their realm.

A resounding, triumphant scream filled the air and we jerked away from each other.

"Shit!" I jumped to my feet and sprinted toward where Eagle had Eve pinned below him.

I waved my arms. "Stop! She's a friend, she'll help us!"

Eagle cocked his head and peered at me, his wounds from her claws already closing over.

Shifting into his human form, he stepped away from the wounded Harpy who sat up, a glazed look on her face. "He's not an eagle?"

I held up my hands, stopping everyone. "He's a Guardian, and so he can shift forms. He's leading us to where the Shamans are being held. Or he was until you two showed up."

Eve looked from me, to Eagle, to O'Shea, and then Alex before sniffing contemptuously, her feathers ruffled. "I could have helped you find the place."

God save me from supernatural egos. "I'm sure you could, but he" —I pointed at Eagle— "was closer. And he's already been there."

O'Shea limped over to me, slipping an arm across my shoulders. "So, where to next?"

Eve blinked twice and her beak dropped open. "How did you survive the fall?"

He shrugged. "Lucky, I guess."

It struck me then that wasn't the only issue he would have been dealing with. "What about you hip? You were cut wide—"

His arm tightened across my shoulders; but he didn't make eye contact. "Wasn't as bad as we thought. Didn't even need stitches. Like I said, I'm just lucky."

Lucky indeed; I felt something in the air shift, tension and secrets felt about the same. O'Shea was keeping something from me, but at that moment, I didn't really care. No, that's not true, I did care; I just didn't have time to deal with it. I would make O'Shea spill his guts. But right now we had to get the Shamans. Not to mention I was running out of time, the fire opal seeming to cool even as I thought about it.

It was decided that with Eve along—relatively unharmed considering the scuffle she and Eagle were in—we would fly the rest of the way, Eve carrying Alex in her claws while O'Shea and I rode on top.

Back in the air, I took stock of the situation. Considering other cases I'd been on, I now had a veritable army of help. But as we swung into view of the ranch, did a low sweep and landed on a rocky outcrop half a mile away, I had a feeling it wasn't going to be enough.

13

Below us, the three remaining Shamans were kneeling in the main courtyard, arms lifted to the sky, smoke billowing around them from the fire pit in front of them. I could see no other people. They were in the center of the ranch, which was laid out like a mini town, multiple buildings, and several open courtyards; none bigger than the one the Shamans were in. Everything about this gave me the heebie jeebies. I couldn't decide if it was the lack of movement down there, or the fact that three powerful Shamans were being held against their will.

"Eagle, can you communicate with your Shaman?"

He shook his head.

"Any chance you know what we're up against?"

His answer was the same as the first.

Shimmying down the rock face, I lowered myself onto a rock ledge, and from there started to slide down the scree.

"Where are you going?" O'Shea asked.

"To get the Shamans."

"Just like that, no plan?"

Pausing, I looked back at him, the scratches no longer bleeding, "Nobody knows why or how they're trapped. I'm going to find out."

Swearing under his breath, he slid down after me, Alex closed in behind him.

"We'll see how close we can get, see if we can break whatever trance they're in," I said.

"What about me?" Eve called after us.

I thought for a moment before speaking. "Circle high, keep the ranch in sight and be ready to do an emergency pick up. You too, Eagle."

The three of us on foot made no effort to hide ourselves from those on the ranch as we approached. No point, there was no cover and it was just past midday, there weren't even any good shadows to use for hiding.

"So," O'Shea said. "We just stroll on up, ask for the Shamans back?"

I didn't miss the sarcasm in his voice. "Yup, pretty much."

"That work for you in the past?"

"Nope, never."

Alex snickered to himself; whether he actually got the humour, I don't know, but I had the feeling he enjoyed seeing me and O'Shea at odds.

O'Shea though, took exception and glared at Alex, his dark eyebrows furrowing. "Shut up, wolf."

Alex cowered as if he'd been hit, hiding as best he could behind my legs. "Sorry, boss."

I frowned at the agent. "Ease up, O'Shea. I need you both to be on your best behavior." Then I gave Alex a look, but I didn't need to. The werewolf was travelling with his head down, tail tucked between his legs. "I be good."

We reached the large gates leading into the courtyard; I stood with my hands resting on the heavy iron bars. "Hello? Anybody home? Avon calling."

The only sound echoing back to me was the low chant of the three Shamans. Again, I wished I understood Navajo.

O'Shea flicked the latch on the gate up, and pushed the panels, opening it with ease.

Motioning for Alex, I pointed at the gate. "You stay here, guard the gate, and howl if you see anyone. Okay?"

Alex nodded, but the spark was gone from his eyes, the jovial werewolf had disappeared under O'Shea's rebuke.

He didn't salute, didn't give me a saucy "Yuppy doody." Nothing. He just sat down, eyes darting from side to side.

"Alex. We won't be long."

Again, nothing.

The chanting stopped and the hairs on my arms and the back of my neck rose in a wave. "We've got to hurry." I took off at a dead run, asking my body to give me more than I knew it had left; I was running on empty. O'Shea ran beside me in an easy lope, not even a hitch from where the bear Guardian had nailed him.

We careened around the final corner and the courtyard opened up. The three Shamans were slumped where they sat, chins to their chests. Shit, they didn't look good. Skin pale under their deep tans, eyes closed, and only the bare flutter of their chests rising and falling. There was a red circle that they sat in, painted on the flagstones. I thought it was the traditional sign of the sun, and only as we drew closer did I see the rays pointed inward. I'd seen a similar design in one of Giselle's books, years ago. The reverse sun was used only when drawing power from someone, sucking it out of them. Not good.

My toe was at the red line, and I pushed it a little further. No sparks, no fireworks.

"O'Shea, get them out to Alex. Flag down Eagle, he can get them back to Louisa's." My throat tightened up, like a noose had settled around it, my entire body going from tense to hyper alert. Where were the bad guys, the ones who'd taken the Shamans?

He bent and picked up the first woman, then jogged her out to the front gate, out of my view. I worked my way around the circle. This was too easy. My skin started to prickle and I circled the courtyard, feeling as though I was missing something. No rescue was ever this easy.

O'Shea came back for the second Shaman and as he lifted her she whispered, her voice hoarse. "Trap. It's a trap."

Startled, I lifted my eyes to O'Shea's. "Get her out of here, now!"

I grabbed the last Shaman, the youngest one who had to be Crystal, under the arms and started to drag her out to the front gate. I didn't want to be here when the trap sprung.

Already though, I knew it was too late. Halfway to the gate the air around us crackled, and a sheen of misty power coalesced around the ranch. Without even touching it I knew it was impenetrable, the power vibrating at a frequency I knew from past experience nothing would get through.

I lowered the Shaman to the ground, propping her against the nearest wall. Right now, she was my only ally and she was out cold. Crystal, the youngest of all four Shamans, and the newest to the calling. Fan-freaking-tastic.

O'Shea stood outside the shimmering power, slamming it with his fists, and then his sword. I could see his mouth moving, but no sound came out. I was truly on my own for this one.

There was no way around it, I would have to go looking for whatever or whomever the power source was coming from and take it out. I smiled, gave O'Shea a thumbs up and headed back toward the courtyard. It was about time I had something to go after, a solid goal. On the edges of my mind, I could feel Ricky waiting for me. There was no time for niceties; the kid had been in the hands of that fucking Troll long enough.

I pulled out both of my swords from my back sheath, swirling them through the air, loosening my muscles. My footsteps echoed weirdly in the courtyard, bouncing off the shimmering power that contained the miniature town.

The courtyard was the same as I'd left it, fire burning hot. I stood next to it, letting the heat warm me, the flames dancing almost as high as my chin. From across the flagstone courtyard, a single figure stepped out of the main doorway. She looked to be in her prime, short cropped black hair, soft brown eyes, and a fit physique for someone who was, on a good day, going to be called short. I doubted she'd come to the middle of my chest, hardly intimidating. She glowered at me, white teeth flashing.

I swirled one sword in the air, cutting through the flames. "*You're* the problem? Well bang me sideways, here I thought I'd be facing down a real bad ass, stealing four Shamans and all."

The petite woman took three steps into the courtyard, her eyes fixated on me. "You have quite the reputation, Rylee." Her words were slurred, almost like she was drunk. Or trying to hide an accent, it was hard to tell.

"Oh joy, it knows my name."

Her face tightened. "I am Jensen. I want you to know my name before I take you and spell you. I will be greatly rewarded for bringing you in."

I laughed, though my heart was starting to beat faster in anticipation for what was coming. "What, there's a bounty out on me now?"

She nodded. "Yes. And I want that bounty. I hear you even took a blow from a demon."

"Doran spilling the beans is he?"

Jensen nodded again, still not smiling.

My jaw clenched. Doran and his big fat mouth were going to get an ass kicking when I was done with her. But if they were on talking terms . . . .

Incredulous, I couldn't help blurting out, "You mean to tell me you're a daywalker?" Of course, once I got rolling I couldn't stop. "You, with the height of a child? You, with the short legs and stubby little arms?

How the fuck did you steal four Shamans? Better yet." I thought of what O'Shea would ask. "Why?"

She didn't nod this time, but the skin around her eyes tightened, as did her lips. Okay, so I'd guessed right. Her body was so still I'd have laid money that she was frozen to the spot.

"You are insolent, aren't you?"

"Well." I shrugged, keeping my body as loose and relaxed as I could. "I've been told that before. I kind of like it. Insolent. Makes me sound like a rebel, don't you think?"

"Those Shamans were easy to steal. They are so full of pride that when I asked for their help, they came. And when I asked for another's help because the first was incapable, they came. Each one too caught up in their own belief that they were the best to realize I'd drawn them in and fooled them."

"Sneaky. Now, I only ask this cause my partner will want to know. Why would you steal them? Want to share?"

I was pushing it, I knew I was. The longer we stood here the better chance she had at getting me to lower my guard.

"Power. They have enough power to help me transition. I only needed two of them. The other two I took so you would be certain to come for them. Do you think it was coincidence that it was Louisa who escaped?"

Hmm. This was not sounding good. I put my hand to my chest, my eyes wide and innocent. "Aw, you did that for me? Remind me to send you flowers."

Jensen snarled. "You little bitch, stop mocking me!"

"Now, little isn't the word I'd use for me. Damn, I'm a freaking behemoth compared to you." I paused, then smiled, a genuine, happy smile I couldn't hold back knowing this would be the word that would send her over the edge. "Squirt."

Okay, maybe that hadn't been the best idea I'd come across, but it was too late now. She rushed me, her face twisting and fangs protruding at a grotesque angle, almost as if her jaw had been broken and reset wrong. That would explain the weird talking.

Two steps from me she slammed on the brakes, and I pointed one sword at her head, the other at her stomach. "Come on then, Happy. Let's get this done."

Her eyes glittered with hatred and madness, not a good combination in my business.

"I am not happy." She snarled at me, lifting one hand up as though she would spell me. Good luck with that.

I couldn't resist.

"Then which dwarf are you?"

Her eyes bulged, and I only had a split second to prep as she threw herself at me, a screaming bundle of fury. Arms wheeling, she seemed to lose control, her eyes rolling back in her head, teeth open and jaw snapping, whatever spell she'd thought to cast forgotten.

I dodged her wild blows easily, dancing away from her, swords arcing through the air, taking off the tips of her fingers on her right hand. Screeching, she leapt, ignoring my weapons. Her mistake.

Two quick thrusts pin cushioned her body, but I would have to take her head if I wanted to end this.

The grimace on her face froze and she stumbled, her fingers clasping her wounds, then the grimace shifted to a smile as she lifted her good hand up, gripping something. I took a deep breath and the cold air sliced through me, dropping me to my knees. I fumbled for the pendant, the fire opal, and found nothing but empty air. There, dangling in Jensen's hand, was the pendant, the leather strap broken.

"Now, you think you are so smart, coming here to kill me; to rescue your friends." Jensen grinned from ear to ear, her teeth looking even worse as a smile than a snarl. Where I'd run her through with my sword gaped at me, two flapping mouths dripping blood, giving me a peek into her innards. But it was if she wasn't hurt, her anger obviously fueling her. "And now you are caught, a prisoner of your pride as they were prisoners of theirs."

"Shit," I mumbled, my lips already going numb as I knelt on the hard stone, the icy blast of winter striking me down. Sure, the venom might not kill me, but Faris was right, the cold damn well could. If nothing else, the cold gave Jensen the edge she needed. Doran hadn't been kidding, with the fire opal gone, the frosted cold sliced through me, a hundred times worse than before.

Laughter echoed around us, and I lifted my eyes to see Jensen, her head thrown back, howling her pleasure.

Teeth chattering, I gave her a thumbs up. "Qu . . . ick think . . . ing, for a runt . . . like . . . you."

Free once more, the demon venom surged through me. In seconds, icicles formed along the tips of my eyelashes and I struggled to move closer to the fire, my mind icing up as fast as my body.

The crackle of the fire drew me closer and I crawled toward it, knowing it was the only chance I had. The flagstones around the fire pit were hot to the touch, and though I knew they would burn me, I laid on them stomach down, soaking in the heat. With the fire burning hot, I might have a chance. Maybe.

Jensen was suddenly standing over me, one of my dropped swords in her hand. "You have really no idea, do you, of what's going on the world? So focused on your 'mission' that you are blind to everything else."

Her words barely made sense to me; the fog of cold that had settled on me was swiftly stealing what was left of my capacities. "Fuck . . . you."

She crouched over me, laying my own sword against my neck, and I was unable to even shift away from her, the blade drawing a line of blood from my skin. The heat from the fire was helping, but not enough to do anything but think—certainly not to retaliate.

Jensen stood, smoothed her hair with her mangled hand, blood dripping from the stumps of her finger-tips. "I will call him, and he will come for you and reward me. What a pleasure it will be to see you chained like the bitch you are. Then I will have my reward. But I think, perhaps, he won't mind if you have been injured, after all. He did only say you must be alive." Her eyes glinted with a feral madness I'd been stupid to underestimate. "And you did attack me."

He? What he? I had a feeling I already knew, but I was so not in the mood for a showdown with Faris, certainly not in this state. Not after the last time we met in person. I had to keep her from calling him, keep her focused on me.

Letting my muscles relax, my left hand slid downward into the fire pit, brushing up against the edge of a burning log, the last quarter of it untouched by the flames. I only had to get my hands on the opal, and I would be able to deal again. My fingers tightened around the warm wood and I curled my upper body around my belly, hiding my hand as best I could.

"I have something . . . for . . . you." I kept my voice soft and meek. Okay, as soft and meek as I could manage.

The daywalker glided toward me, once more bending over my body, my sword tip pressing between my shoulder blades. It was a chance I was willing to take.

"What is it, *little* Tracker?"

I fought the cold. It spooled out of my chest, shutting down my ability to move, to think, to act. But there wouldn't be another chance like this.

With a scream of anger, and a burst of energy I knew I wouldn't be able to repeat, I flung the burning log upward, smashing Jensen in the face. The tip of my sword started to penetrate my back, and then was pinned down as I rolled.

She screamed, her hands on her face, the opal slipping from her fingers. It bounced once and rolled away from us both. Shit, shit, shit!

While Jensen screamed, the flames eating away at her face, I struggled to my knees, my hands turning to lumps of ice as I crawled away from the fire pit. Three feet away from the glimmering stone fingers bit into my legs, stopping me in my pitiful tracks.

"Oh, no you don't," Jensen said, her voice sloppy, face partially melted like a wax candle gone awry. Her head snapped down and she buried her fangs into my calf.

Screaming, I booted her in the head with my other leg, fear overcoming the cold for a split second. I had a vision of her taking my blood and, with it, the demon venom, creating a monster I knew I would have no chance of stopping. I couldn't let that happen. Her teeth unlatched and she reared her head for another blow. I lurched forward, dragging her with me, my fingers circling around the opal.

Heat rushed through me, freeing my muscles from the bindings of the venom, pushing it back. I kicked her in the face, then scrambled to my feet, my body once more my own.

Opal gripped in one hand, I scooped my sword off the ground, took two strides and was standing over Jensen.

"You picked the wrong girl to bite." I brought the sword down in a perfect arc, taking Jensen's head in a shower of blood and gristle.

With my boot, I shoved her body into the fire, a whoosh of flames shooting up to the sky as they engulfed her body. Her head, I left out. Breathing hard, I gripped the opal, wondering if I could hug Doran and kick his ass at the same time. I didn't know if it was possible, but I was going to try.

14

"**R**yleeeee!" Alex came galloping into the square, bowling into my legs, grabbing at me with a frantic need. I pushed him off me, gently, but with a firm insistence.

"Hey, buddy." I cleaned off my sword and slid it back into its sheath, then picked up my other one and did the same. O'Shea was right behind the werewolf, sword bared, eyes taking in the scene in one sweep. He didn't lower his blade though, instead keeping it bared and ready.

"Adamson?"

"Yeah, I'm okay." My leg ached where Jensen bit me, my back stung where my blade had bit in, and my body was still humming with the transition from freezing cold to hot, but she was dead and I wasn't. Good all around.

O'Shea made a move as if to hug me and I stiffened up. "I said I'm okay."

"You've got blood on your back." He spun me around for a better look. "It doesn't look too deep."

"Yeah, it's fine."

Now he did hug me, from behind where I couldn't get away, the warmth of his body eas-

ing through mine. I relaxed into him for a brief
second, and then shot a look at Alex who just sat
there, tongue lolling, eyes wide and innocent as
ever. He waved at me, but made no move as if he
were upset. What had happened while I was locked
in with the daywalker?

As if reading my mind, O'Shea whispered in my
ear. "Alex and I had a chat."

I stiffened up. "You didn't hurt him, I hope." O'Shea
let go of me, going right back to business.

"Let's go."

It didn't take long to cue up Eagle and Eve, bringing
them down to scoop up the remaining Shamans and
Alex.

"Rylee, I can take you all if you like. I can pick up a
five hundred pound cow, so a few puny humans are
nothing."

I shook my head. "O'Shea and I will wait here. I
want to do a walkthrough of this place anyway," I
said, catching O'Shea's nod out the corner of my eye.

They left in a flurry of wings and wind. O'Shea and
I would have about an hour to see what we could find.
I was cutting it close with the fire opal, but it would be
worth it if we could find out what the hell Jensen was
really up to. And if Faris was involved.

I let him lead the way for once, my body sore, and
to be honest, something was different about him. I
couldn't pin it down, but I wanted to watch him, see
if I could figure it out.

Barely pausing in the threshold of the doorway,
O'Shea strode into the main building, the one Jensen
had stepped out of.

"Be careful. She might have had other traps, or minions working for her."

"Minions?"

"I like the sound of it better than slaves."

We both went silent as we made our way deeper into the adobe building. The walls were thick, and the air no warmer than outside. More than that, the rooms were empty of anything. No furnishings, paintings. It was like it had been abandoned years ago. My skin prickled with awareness as I took a deep breath, the scent of incense long burnt out lingering in the air.

"I'm not seeing anything," O'Shea said, stopping in the middle of the fourth room we'd come to.

"Yeah, but that doesn't mean there isn't anything here." I let my eyes slide to half-mast, focusing on my second sight. The world around me flickered and I could see there were a few things hidden from view. We worked our way back through the rooms we'd already come through, and though there was an item here or there, there was nothing of substance until we were back to the main room. A large hand-hewn table dominated the middle of the room, an oversized, leather bound book lying in the middle of it.

I picked the book up and let go of my second sight, pulling the book with me across to the seen world.

"What the . . . ?" O'Shea asked, coming to peer over my shoulder.

It looked like a journal. I flipped through the pages, reading the flowing script with only a little difficulty.

"She was trying to become a vampire in truth," I said, turning the pages, the story becoming clearer the more I read. "She was going to use the power from the

Shamans to transition from daywalker to vampire. And she was bound to serve . . ." I didn't say Faris' name out loud. But there it was on the paper. Jensen had been one of his.

"Is that even possible?"

That was a good question, one that was eating at me. If Jensen had succeeded there would have been a gold rush of sorts set off. Daywalkers were a jealous, power hungry bunch to begin with. If they thought they could become their bigger, badder, more powerful cousins, no Shaman would be safe. Of course, that was assuming Jensen's recipe was legit.

"I don't know," I said, turning another page, fingers gripping the book hard when I read the words on it. This was bad news, in so many ways.

O'Shea said it for me. "Looks like the final ingredient was you."

That was not good. I tore the damning pages out of the book.

He put a hand out, "What are you doing, that's evidence?"

I shook the pages at him, "Yeah, evidence my blood could help a daywalker become a vampire. You think that's going to help me live a long and fruitful life?"

Folding the sheets up, I jammed them into my inside coat pocket. "The last thing I need is to become a target." The sound of wings brought my head around. "There's our ride. Let's get out of here."

The agent didn't say anything else. Smart man. I grabbed the large book, tucking it under my arm. I wanted a chance to have a more thorough read through, when I wasn't on a salvage or full of demon venom.

The ride back to Louisa's was a non-event, thank God for small mercies. Once we landed at her place though, the non-event turned into a knockdown, drag out fight. But for once, I wasn't in it.

The four Shamans were screaming at each other; Louisa had her hand wrapped in Crystal's hair and was shaking her like a dog with a bone.

The two Guardians were standing back, watching the Shamans as if the women were having tea, not fisticuffs.

"Um, anyone going to break this up?" I asked, sliding from Eve's back.

Bear raised his eyebrows at me. "Would you like to get between them?"

"No, but I need them," I said, striding as best I could toward the four women. They weren't speaking English, I think they were speaking Navajo, so I had no idea what the fight was about. The thing that worried me the most was the current of power circling around them, as if it were building up. Apparently, Louisa had been right and their powers had been returned to them with Jensen dead. I tried to talk over them, asked nicely. Waved my arms. They ignored me. Well, there was one sure way to get their attention.

"Louisa, get your friends under control; you four owe me."

They stilled as a group, four sets of eyes turning to stare at me in disbelief.

"We owe you?" Louisa asked, her voice deceptively sweet. I smiled at her, cocked a hip and folded my arms across my chest, leather jacket creaking.

"Not only do you owe me, I intend for you to owe me for some time. Each of you." I pointed to them one at a time.

Louisa sniffed. "I owe you nothing."

I took a step toward her, anger sparking deep in my belly. "You would go back on your words? What if I hadn't killed the daywalker, what then? You'd be nothing. Just a human with a good story."

She gasped as if I'd struck her across the face.

The negotiations began in earnest then. I'd known it would come down to this. Even though I'd pulled their asses out of the fire, they would bargain with me how much it was worth to them.

We settled on two favors per Shaman, plus a question each. Maybe that doesn't sound like a lot, but when it comes to Shamans. each thing you receive from them is costly. I'd gotten a landslide of bonuses for breaking them all free of the daywalker.

"How'd she catch you, anyway?" I asked.

The Shamans blushed a deep scarlet, and Louisa raised her hand. "It is an embarrassment that it even happened. We were prideful and foolish. That is enough, do not ask us again."

Someone behind us cleared his throat. O'Shea lifted his eyebrows at me. "Let's make this happen."

"Working on it," I said, frowning at him. Since when did he get his knickers in a knot about hurrying things up?

"Ladies, I need to ask to use one of my favors from each of you. Right now."

Except for Louisa, they all looked surprised, but they nodded. I took a breath and said, "I need you to help me purge the demon venom I've got stuck in me."

Louisa smiled and the other Shamans nodded, though I could see Crystal's eyes widen briefly before she hid her emotions.

"Of course," Louisa said. "We will do so immediately. It will take a little time to prepare."

I pursed my lips and lifted one hand in the air. "There is one other thing."

The four Shamans stared at me, but again it was Louisa who spoke. "Another favor?"

"No. Doran will assist. It was the price I had to pay for his help. He gets the venom when it is extracted."

A collective intake of breath by the four women held my attention. They exchanged glances, their hands flashing as they signed to one another.

Louisa's eyes had gone from the silver of before back to the dark brown I'd first met her with, brows drawn over them and the corners of her lips tipped downward. Yeah, I didn't think having Doran involved would make them too happy. Especially not after being snatched by a daywalker. Too bloody bad.

"Since you have already convinced us to help you, we will do this. But you are pushing the limits of our patience, Tracker." Never good when a Shaman calls you by your title and not your name.

I shrugged. "That's how the shit hits the fan."

The four women dispersed with strict instructions to stay where I was. Fine by me. I made my way up to the back porch, slumped into a chair, put Jensen's book on my lap, and closed my eyes. Tracking Ricky was easy, and I breathed a sigh of relief; his heart still beat, and while he continued to sleep, for now at least he was alright. I just hoped he could hang on for one more day.

"You sure you're okay?" O'Shea sat down beside me, the wicker chair creaking under him. The faint musk of wolf and bear wisped around me. I opened my eyes. "I'm fine, but what's up with you?"

He pulled back, seemingly offended. "What do you mean? Other than pissed off that you won't trust me, that you won't let me help you?" Standing up, he pointed into the house. "Inside, where we aren't going to be overheard." Yeah, like everyone outside wouldn't hear us screaming at each other. Right.

I didn't have the strength to fight him on this, not today.

We wove our way through almost to the front of the house, his hand on my elbow, guiding me until he found a spare room. I tossed the book onto the bed. Shutting the door, he turned me to face him. Okay, time to grow up and be an adult about this.

I stared up at him. "Tell me the real reason you're helping me. You spent years thinking I was a criminal, and now you've got a girlfriend, why are you still hanging around?"

He frowned, confusion marring his features and clouding his eyes. "A girlfriend? I'm not seeing anyone."

Damn, he was going to make me say it. I cleared my throat and waved a hand in the air. "Milly. I know you two are . . ." I waved my hands in the air bumping them against each other, still not able to say it. So much for being an adult.

His eyebrows shot into his hairline and just as quickly swept down into a frown. "You think I'm sleeping with Milly? Are you out of your mind?"

I let myself step back. "The two of you, after India was taken home . . . ." I never got to finish my sentence. In a flash of movement I could have avoided if I wasn't so damn tired, he was on me.

O'Shea pinned me against the wall, his hands wrapped around my wrist, body pressing into mine. Not necessarily a bad thing.

"What do you think you saw between me and your skanky so-called friend?"

Jaw tight, I did my best to ignore the flush of heat between us, the lust that tightened my muscles and begged for me to slide my fingers over his skin. Nope, couldn't happen. Unless, of course, I was wrong about him and Milly? Hope slid through me and I pushed it away. I'd seen the lipstick on his skin, seen the way she'd looked at him.

"It's not what I thought I saw. You two went for coffee, I know what that means . . ."

He cut me off again, his mouth dangerously close to mine. "You saw me ask her to call me. To talk about the case, about India's case. That's it. You might not care why the Coven took the kid, but it's my job to find out why. Milly was my best shot at figuring out the motive. She understands witches; I don't."

I wanted to believe him, but I knew my friend. She wouldn't let a man like O'Shea slip past her, not even for me.

"Men don't talk to Milly. It's not what she's known for when it comes to her mouth." I shifted my weight.

If I wanted to get away, I could; but really, I didn't want to end this moment.

O'Shea's lips hovered over mine, the feel of his breath against my skin, and I fought the desire to lean into him. All it would take was a simple tilt of my head to taste him once more.

Dark eyes searched mine, a look of confusion filling them before he gave me a smile, soft and oh-so-tender. His fingers on my wrists were gentle, circling the sensitive skin and sending a shiver of lust through me.

"You mean to tell me that from one phone call, and a single coffee meeting, you deduced Milly and I were sleeping together?" He let out a low laugh, "That's not very good detective work, when you didn't even interrogate the suspects."

"She had love bites. And you had lipstick on your neck," I said, spitting it out before I thought better of it.

He whispered his next words, barely breathed out they were so quiet, deep and husky, his lips brushed against my own.

"Rylee, it's not Milly's mouth I want."

I stared up at him, barely daring to breathe. Whatever chills I'd been feeling were gone, his body pressed against me radiated heat and desire. Shit, now what? O'Shea's dark eyes beckoned to me, his hands working their way up to my shoulders, slipping underneath my jacket and pushing it off my body.

Ah, screw it.

Reaching up, I closed the miniscule distance between us, our lips meeting with a soft groan, his or mine, I had no idea. With one swift move, O'Shea picked me up and I wrapped my legs around his waist, jacket dropping to the floor. His arousal throbbed against me as his hands worked my shirt off. With a frustrated growl, he yanked my shirt over my head, eyes full of desire. For me, not for Milly. I was so focussed on the sensations, the desire, the play of his hands on my skin, I didn't hear the knock on the door.

He pulled away from me and I whimpered. I actually fucking *whimpered*.

"Yeah?"

"We are ready for Rylee now. Bring her out. And don't bother putting your clothes on, Rylee. We need you naked. There is a robe on the back of the door."

Great. My face heated and I stared at the ground in an attempt to get my body under control. Slow even breaths helped, but when O'Shea, Liam, began to strip me out of the rest of my clothes, my heart picked back up.

"Stop, I can do this myself," I said, giving him a half-hearted push away. He grinned up at me and nipped the skin on my side. A shot of adrenaline zinged through me. "I mean it." Gods, my voice was breathy, this was ridiculous.

Laughing softly, Liam stood, and even turned his back to me. "It's not like I haven't seen you in your bare skin before."

"Not the point," I said, stepping out of my jeans and stripping down to the buff. The only thing I left on was the fire opal, the stone nestled in the hollow of my throat. Liam shifted to let me reach past him for the robe, his eyes tracing my body.

"Damn. Timing sucks," he said, his voice husky.

Laughing softly, I slipped on the robe and cinched it around my waist. "You're telling me."

15

"**Y**ou must choose someone to go with you. Someone you can trust."

Crap, I'd forgotten about that part. It was bad enough I needed the Shamans to help me, bad enough that Doran was sitting off to the side, smirking at me in my thin robe, his opal hanging from my neck.

"I'll go with her," Liam said, and before I could say yes or no, he shrugged out of his coat and pulled his shirt over his head.

Doran gave a low whistle, eyes dilating as he stared at Liam's bare chest. "Lucky girl."

"Shut up, Doran, you are here only because you must be," Louisa said, her voice firm and calm, but her eyes flashed. With her powers back, she was no longer the meek woman who'd sat crumpled on her back porch. Now she was the Shaman I remembered: tall, imposing, and in control.

Doran smiled, a glint of fangs at the edge of his lips. "Remember you called me, Louisa."

"Only because you must be here to help Rylee. No other reason." She said, glaring at him.

Louisa directed the other Shamans to the four points of the compass around the lodge that, by the smoke billowing out of it, was heating up nicely. Her instructions were all in Navajo, so I turned to Doran. "What should I expect?"

A flash of fangs as he smiled at me did not soothe my worries. "Pain, a lot of pain."

Well, that sounded absolutely fantastic.

The male Shaman continued to smile as he spoke. "After the venom is lanced, you will sleep for some time. We will leave you on your own until the fires die down." He beckoned to Liam and handed him a cut glass flask.

"Here, you will need this to collect the venom." Liam took the flask without a word.

Louisa came back to stand with Doran, singing a chant under her breath as she waved eagle feathers over my face. Smooth, like silk, they slid over my bare skin, tickling and tracing designs. Finishing her chant, Crystal took her place, and sang her chant over me, stroking me with feathers as well. Each of the Shamans did this until they were all back where they'd started, at the four points of the lodge.

Doran stood at the doorway, hands clasped behind his back. With a mocking bow, he gestured for me to go through the hide door. "When you're ready."

"Aren't you going to sing for me?" I asked, lifting an eyebrow.

His face was serious for the first time since I'd met him, and he gave me a slow answer. "When it's time, I will sing."

I took a deep breath; not afraid, but anxious. There was the possibility this wouldn't work. Why would I think that? Because that's life, and rarely do things go as planned.

With his hand held out to me, I knew what Doran wanted. The fire opal.

Reluctantly, I reached around to untie the knot in the leather cord, holding the stone for a moment in my hand before dropping it into the Shaman's.

The cold hit me like a hammer blow, but before I could fall to the ground, Liam scooped me up and pushed through the doorway into the sweat lodge.

The heat, as intense as it was, as suffocating as it felt, barely touched the cold lancing through my body. Shivering violently, it was more like a seizure than being cold. My limbs flailed, body bucked as if electricity passed through it. Liam laid me down on a plush pile of robes, the scent of incense and sage floating up around me. A hint of wolf mingled with them and I stared at a gray pelt beneath my shaking fingers.

"Stay with me, Rylee," Liam said, stretching out beside me, his presence calming me even as I shivered hard enough to make my eyes blur.

I couldn't answer him, could only concentrate on the ice spreading through my limbs, making it hard to breathe as it crushed my chest in its vice-like grip. Outside the lodge the chanting grew, rising and falling, but ever growing to the point where I could no longer hear my teeth chattering, or my heart beating.

The women's voices blended, harmonizing as they laid their spell on the venom, drawing it out of me, forcing the demon to relinquish its hold. *Fuck*, it hurt!

Liam's hands stroked my face, my shoulders, my back as I writhed on the robes, the fire burning hot beside us as he added more fuel, but still, it wasn't enough to chase back the frozen ice flow in my blood. The scent of fresh cut wood overpowered the sage and I breathed deep, groaning as the air escaped me. Never had I felt pain like this. It exploded through me, bombs set over nerve endings to incapacitate me. Through it all, Liam held me, speaking to me, lips moving, though I couldn't hear him; the chanting all my ears could handle.

In a sudden arc of sound, the women's voices were joined by a man's deep baritone, rumbling through their higher notes. Doran was adding his power to Louisa and the other Shamans. Like taking a knife, his voice stabbed into my chest, dug around and drew out the venom. The combined flow of strength cut through the cold, and the venom fought back, using my body as a battlefield. Sharp icicles jabbed my insides, stabbing at my lungs, heart, stomach, and kidneys. I bit down on my lower lip to stop the building screams, focusing on the chanting I could still hear. Rising in crescendo and depth, the Shamans continued to pull on the venom, but it was if they were tugging on a piece of me, pulling my body inside out.

The venom roared within me, cracking through my pores, freezing over my thighs as if they were chunks of wood. Doran's voice changed in pitch and intensity, anger flowing through him into me; a pure fight between the Shaman and the demon. A new sound split the air, shocking me. My screams overpowered everything and my body arced into a perfect curve, heels and the top of my head the only things touching the robes I lay on, as Doran's voice rippled through me, seeking the venom, forcing it out. Seconds drew into minutes as his voice pierced through the venom, unhooking it from my body and making it do his bidding. If I hadn't been in so much pain, I would have been impressed.

The cool edge of the flask was against my breastbone—Liam doing his job—the ice pouring out of me in a viscous black and blue stream. Throat raw, I whimpered as the last of it slipped out of my body, the mark of the demon still on my skin, though its venom was gone. The perfect black snowflake clung to me, a reminder of what had almost happened.

A soft breath of relief escaped my lips, my body collapsed into the robes, and I passed out.

Rylee slumped into the robes, her skin flushing pink almost as soon as he corked the cut glass flask. Putting the last of the wood on the fire, O'Shea lay down beside her, his hands tracing over her shoulders to her lower back, tugging her close.

His neck and shoulders were tense, and the chanting was still coiling around him, like a rope tightening. Ducking his head, he tucked his face into the hollow of Rylee's throat, breathing in her scent. Notes of jasmine, sage, and wolf musk mingled on her skin, and he let out a low rumble in his chest. Unable to stop himself, he put his lips to her skin, flicking his tongue out along the beading sweat. Groaning, he closed his eyes and tightened his hold on her.

Images flashed through his mind, scenes he'd never seen, moments he'd never lived. Blood, snow, moon and stars, torn flesh, and the roar of a beast hovered just under his skin. Swallowing the images down, he struggled to understand what was happening. His fingers traced the nearly invisible scars the Guardian had inflicted on his hip. Was that what had happened? Was he becoming a shifter? His eyes flashed open, staring at the top of the lodge.

No!

He was human, not some freak of nature. This was nothing more than a virus, some weird hallucination from the herbs that were in the sweat lodge. That made sense. Of course it did. His heart ceased its sudden frantic pounding, and again he closed his eyes, though the distant howl of the wild sung to him in his dreams.

Sleep eased from me, like a blanket being drawn off my naked body. I was warm all over, my breath easy in my chest and the heavy weight of a man's arm slung over my waist. I didn't have a single ache forming from the expulsion of the venom. In fact, even the wounds Jensen gave me had healed. Now that was a sweet deal.

Rolling to my side, I stared down at Liam, his eyes still closed, his breathing even. He'd stayed with me the whole night. My heart jumped and I looked over my shoulder to see the coals were still hot, a flame flickering here and there.

The Shamans *had* said I needed to stay in until the fire went out. Well then, I'd just have to find some way to spend the time productively.

A wicked sense of naughtiness stole over me, and I scooted my body closer to Liam. Using just the tips of my fingers, I swirled a path down his chest to the tops of his thighs and back up again. He let out a moan that made my muscles clench in anticipation.

Continuing my exploration, I traced the edges of his muscles through his stomach, chest and arms.

"Are you trying to drive me crazy?" His hands covered mine.

I smiled up at him. "Maybe."

With a soft growl, he flipped me onto my back. The reverberation echoed from his chest into mine, and I shivered, feeling the tension between us grow thick with wanting each other.

He lay over me, his skin a heat that rivalled the flames beside us; I squirmed underneath him, watching his eyes dilate.

Dropping his mouth to mine, he kissed me as if he would devour me whole, and I returned the sentiment. Nipping at my lips, he pulled back, and then proceeded to start his own exploration over my body. Shoulders, neck, belly, and inner thighs. It was like he was avoiding all the sweet spots. On purpose.

I gripped his broad shoulders, digging my nails into his skin as I arched under his mouth, tried to align him with what I wanted his lips on. He laughed softly. "Impatient?"

"You are such a tease," I whispered.

"Just returning the favor."

With a groan, I gave up trying to make him do anything and just surrendered to the sensations. Skin on skin, it was the first time in a long time I'd felt so connected to someone; so safe. His mouth moved over me, hands trailing paths of burning fire as he teased my body into a trembling mass of muscle and flesh.

I grabbed his hair and pulled him upward, tired of waiting. Taking his lips, I kissed him hard, begging him between breaths.

"Please, Liam, please."

He didn't listen, just continued on at a pace that drove me out of my mind with wanting him. Kissing his way down my throat he bit lightly along the edge of my collarbone, finally making his way to the edge of my breast.

My body screamed with desire, and I loved every second of it. Still, I didn't want him to think he was going to have all the fun. With a quick twist I flipped him onto his back, and straddled his hips. "You are going too slow."

He smiled up at me, dark eyes full of desires I could hardly wait to taste. "And you are going too fast."

I ran my hands down his chest, feeling each exquisite inch of muscle tremble under my fingertips. Resting my hands on the waistband of his pants, I shimmied backwards, taking his pants with me.

"These are seriously in the way." I flipped the clothes behind me. He gave a low growl of pleasure, the sound rippled along my spine and sent a delicious shiver through my body. My eyes went to his hip, were the Guardian has slashed him open. The wound was already closed up, healing as if it had been weeks and not a few days. Lucky indeed, the power the Shamans had drawn up must have spilled over into him helping him heal fast.

Liam sat up, wrapped his arms around my waist and pulled me tight against him, redirecting my flow of thoughts. Hovering just above him on my knees, the feel and throb of his erection pressed against the tight warmth between my legs. I tipped my hips toward him, brushing against his erection, shuddering at how close we were. Liam's eyes closed and he let out a low groan. "You really are a tease." I moved to take him into me, but he put his hands on my hips to keep me from sliding down onto his shaft. "Not yet, Rylee. There's no hurry, the fire is a long ways from out."

I glanced at the fire pit, saw the dying embers. "Actually—"

The look in his eyes struck me. He wasn't talking about the fire pit. He was talking about us.

"Oh."

Rolling to the side he took me with him, the length of our bodies fitting together in a simple movement I felt helpless against; but not in a way that freaked me out. There was no denying this, and for once I wouldn't try.

Feeling bold, I slid my hand down between our bodies, slipping past his erection to cup him, squeezing ever so slightly. A sharp hiss of breath escaped his lips. I smiled thinking I was in charge, the one running this sexy show. Not so much.

He dipped his head and took one nipple gently between his teeth, drawing it into the deep warmth of his mouth, his other hand teasing along the edges of my inner thigh until he pressed his fingers into me, swirling in the heat that was building between my legs.

Gasping, I arched into him, all thoughts of being in charge fleeing my brain. Unable to stop myself, I thrust my hips into his hands, noises I barely recognized slipping out of me. Heat, desire, the smell of Liam's skin; I shivered with the whirlwind that rose within me, bursts of lightning seemingly dancing along my skin as my body bucked under his hands and mouth.

"Liam, please," I begged, feeling the need to finish this with him.

With a groan, he gave in, sliding into me with a single smooth thrust and I wrapped my legs around his waist almost jerking him into me, our bodies moving together, a dance as old as time.

We rode the momentum, our skin slick with sweat, breath coming in short sharp gasps as we rode the wave, cresting at the top together. Trembling, he held himself slightly above me, staring down into my eyes.

"That was worth the wait."

I smiled up at him, my body singing his praises. "You bet your sweet ass it was."

Laughing, we collapsed on the pile of furs, but I kept my legs wrapped around his waist when he made a move to get off me.

"Where do you think you're going?" I asked, sweetly, batting my eyelashes up at him.

Laughing softly, he shook his head, bending to nip at my ear. "Absolutely nowhere."

16

Doran was waiting for me as I stepped out of the sweat lodge, robe gripped around my waist. The grin spread across his face. "If I'd known what the morning's activities were going to be, I'd have offered to go in with you."

Crap, did that mean everyone knew? The four female Shamans were sitting on the back porch, smiling out my way. Apparently so. I wasn't ashamed, it was just, well, your first time with someone, you don't exactly want a welcoming committee afterward.

"Was he any good? I didn't hear any screaming after *I* was done with you." Doran smirked, and I did the only thing I could think of.

I punched him in the nose. The cartilage crunched under my fist, and Doran wheeled away, laughing and yelping. Yes, I said laughing.

"Bitch, I'm glad I didn't bed you. You Trackers. So God-damned touchy!"

"That's for talking to Jensen, you ass."

Liam stepped out behind me, his pants and shirt on, even if the shirt was un-buttoned. I clenched my robe against the sharp, winter wind. It was cold, but

I didn't feel like anything was going to kill me. Running barefoot across the frosted ground, I leapt up the stairs and raced to the back bedroom.

Closing the door behind me, I was surprised to see Alex passed out on his back, snoring loudly. Grabbing my clothes, I started to pull them on, calling to the werewolf.

"Alex, come on, we've got to get going."

He startled awake, rolling off the bed with a thump. Peeking up at me over the edge, he lifted his nose and sniffed the air.

"Rylee mates the boss?"

Scrunching my face up, I nodded. If he thought Liam was the boss, all the better. "Yes."

Snorting once, he scratched at his butt with his claws, pulling them out to give them a sniff before saying anything. "Okey dokey."

That was it? Damn, I'd been expecting a full-out war again with him growling at Liam and me trying to step between them. This was good, life was looking up.

I paused in dressing to reach for Ricky, Tracking him easily. Still asleep. That was too weird. Though I preferred him not to have to see whatever the dumb ass Troll was up to, I didn't like that he had been unconscious for so long.

Gathering up my weapons, I strapped everything down and headed back out into the main house. Louisa was there, talking quietly with Liam.

"Keep an eye on her. If for one instant"—she held a pointy finger up to his nose—"you think there is a speck of the venom left, you bring her back to us."

The agent nodded, his dark hair tousled with sleep, but his eyes were keen and alert. I fought back the—what I knew would be goofy—smile from my lips.

"Thank you Louisa," I said.

"You're welcome."

Silence, then; no 'thank you' would be forthcoming from her. Shaking my head, I touched Liam on the arm. "We should go. Ricky is waiting on us."

Eve was waiting outside, her head dropped so she could speak with Eagle. We approached them, not making any effort to hide ourselves, but still, Eve jumped when we got close.

"Rylee, you are well?"

"I am. Can you take us back to the Landing Pad?"

She bobbed her head once, glanced at Eagle, and then lowered herself so Liam and I could climb on. Again, Alex would ride in her claws.

As we lifted from the ground, Eagle gave a shrill cry and Eve answered it with one of her own. She made swift time though, between Louisa's and Dox's place, the wind blowing in our favor.

Dox came rushing out, and I gave him a double thumbs up. Scooping me up into his arms, he gave me his trademark bone-crushing hug. Or at least, he started to. I was yanked out of his arms and shoved behind Liam so hard I actually stumbled.

"What the hell is wrong with you?" I shoved the agent.

He turned to me, his eyes wild, skin flushed as though with fever. Shit, maybe he had an infection? No, the sweat lodge would have helped with that.

Dox though, didn't seem bothered, not at all. He took a look at O'Shea, a look at me, and threw his head back with a bellowing laugh. "Shit, I didn't think you'd actually bed him, Rylee!"

O'Shea didn't move, but something shifted in him, a tensing of muscles, a moment of pressure in the air. I lifted my hand. "Don't ruin this, not now, not here." Of course, the minute I sleep with the guy, he gets all weird and possessive.

This was the last thing I needed, and yet my heart stumbled almost as much as my feet had. I'd thought, for a brief second, O'Shea was different. That he wouldn't be an ass. What was I thinking?

O'Shea shook himself, a tremor rippling through him, and he finally turned to face Dox. I couldn't see the look that passed between them, but I could guess. He grunted a "Sorry" at the ogre and then brushed past him, through the motel and right out the other side.

Dox clapped a hand on my shoulder. "Don't be too hard on him. When he's ready, he'll tell you."

"Tell me what?"

The ogre just smiled at me, but didn't pull me back into a hug. Eve cleared her throat. "Rylee, I must ask you something."

Ruffling her feathers, the Harpy ducked her head. "I would like to stay here for some time. Eagle has agreed to train me. But not forever, I would come back to you, in a few months."

This would be good for her, to train with someone who could fly with her. And it would keep Milly from harping—bad pun, I know—at me.

"Are you sure," I asked, not wanting her to think I was happy she was staying, though a part of me was sighing a large breath of relief.

"Yes, I'm sure."

I gave her a nod, and headed toward the front of the building. "You did good, Eve. Just come home when you're ready."

She gave a screech that made the hair on my body stand at attention, and then a whoosh of wind curled around me as she launched into the air.

"Keep an eye out for her, Dox," I said, striding through the building.

"Of course, and you take care of yourself, Rylee."

Deliberately, within sight of O'Shea and the SUV, I turned and hugged Dox, keeping one eye on the agent. His jaw tightened and his hands flexed on the steering wheel, but at least he didn't get out of the vehicle.

"Always pushing the boundaries," Dox muttered, patting me on the back. "Get out of here, before you start a brawl."

I laughed, but my heart was feeling bruised at being such a bad judge of character. I didn't think jealous was a word I could have applied to O'Shea, and wouldn't have until he yanked me away from Dox. "You'd squash him like an overripe melon."

Dox's face sobered. "I wouldn't be so sure of that." Giving me a little shove in the direction of the SUV, he waved at Alex who was already in the back of the vehicle, bouncing like crazy.

Good times, just me, a werewolf, and a cranky, jealous FBI agent on an eighteen-hour run back to North Dakota, most likely through a snowstorm.

Good times indeed.

He drove as if he were alone, silent and staring straight ahead. The snowstorms that had chased them south had eased off, and the driving was simple enough. So what was his problem? How about the wild rage that had gripped him when the ogre hugged Rylee? O'Shea was not a possessive man, never in his life had jealousy been something he'd had to deal with. But it was like a light switch had been flicked on and his only thought was to tear off the arms of the one who was holding her.

That was not a good sign. And with each mile they drove in silence, the gap between them widened. He thought about her sweet pleas as she writhed underneath him, whispering his name as they clung to each other. Now, she wouldn't even look at him.

"If you're going to yell at me, just do it. I know I was an ass." He said, gritting his teeth as the admission fell from his lips.

"Dox is one of my closest friends. I will damn well hug him if I want to." She snapped, her eyes flashing as she pinned him to the seat with her gaze. "You think because we had sex, you have ultimate say in my life?" She rested her head in one hand. "Fuck, what was I thinking?"

That stung.

He took a slow breath, breathing in her scent, as if that alone could tell him what to say. She was hurt, and angry. A trickle of fear tickled his nose. Fear? How could he smell that?

Swallowing hard, he said nothing, his own fear rising up around him like a fog. Agent Valley had been right; O'Shea should never have slept with Rylee. No, that was a lie—he'd do it again in an instant.

"How's the kid?"

Rylee closed her eyes briefly. "Sleeping."

"Still?"

"Yeah, I know. Even drugged, I haven't felt him even sort of wake up, not once."

Alex bounced in the back seat, and O'Shea gave him a frown. Slinking, the werewolf slumped into his seat. "No fairseezz."

Rylee turned in her seat. "What's no fair?"

Alex pointed at O'Shea. "Boss man."

She looked from the werewolf to O'Shea, then back again, her eyes taking in more than O'Shea was comfortable with. He wasn't sure he knew what was going on; he sure as hell didn't want her figuring it out first.

"You want to tell me something," she asked.

This was it; this was the moment to tell her what he was afraid of, what he suspected had happened. She would understand, of all the people in his life, she would be the one to get it.

He stared out at the landscape they were passing through, the snow sparkling in the sun.

"Nope."

The slight grind of her teeth was the only thing that tipped him off. And how the hell could he hear that anyway, it was quieter than a mouse's fart? Clamping down on the emotions that roared through him, he fought the fear. This was a battle that had nothing to do with her, and there was nothing she could do to help.

So why did it feel like he was betraying her with his silence?

17

North Dakota was socked in, the whole freaking state a complete white out. Apparently, it hadn't been *all* my and the demon venom's fault that winter had come early.

As we drove into Bismarck, the feeling of Ricky in my head intensified, his heart beating steady and rhythmical. That, at least, was a good sign.

"Where are we going first?" O'Shea asked. No longer was I thinking of him as Liam, the sweet, generous lover who'd watched over me in the sweat lodge. Nope, he was relegated back to being the asshole agent who stuck around just to watch me fail.

Though I did have to give him a small amount of credit. One of the few things I could say I liked about the FBI agent at this moment was that he listened to me and followed my lead when it came to the supernatural. I had no doubt *that* would change once he got his legs under him in my world. But for now, it was super handy.

"We go after Ricky. It's been too long already and I've got most of the things we need in my bag. We're only another ten minutes away." I curled in my seat, focusing on the kid. I couldn't believe with all the detours and time we'd had to take, we were still going to make it to him before that asshat of a Troll did anything. I had to believe that.

"Do you have a plan?"

Yeah, that was the sticky part of this. What O'Shea didn't know, but would soon enough, was that Trolls rarely worked alone. Sure, I'd duped the dumb ass, one-eyed bastard before, but that had been only one. How the hell was I supposed to extricate a kid from a raging angry Troll, and all his friends?

So I fudged. "Working on it."

O'Shea looked in the mirror, his eyes full of the disbelief I knew I deserved.

Adamson was not a happy girl. The vibes rolling off her stated more than words and O'Shea knew it was his fault. He should have just told her what he suspected.

Damn it, even now his mouth was all but glued shut.

He kept his hands tight on the steering wheel, stalling his desire to reach over and touch her, assure himself she was still with him. That he hadn't messed up so badly that they couldn't come back from it.

They came up to an intersection and he slowed down. "Adamson?"

"Well, at least we're in agreement on what we're calling each other," she muttered, probably thinking he couldn't hear her. "Go straight," she said, in a louder voice.

He did as she said, ignoring the fact that the road he was going straight on was a one way. With the weather, there weren't many people out on the roads anyway. He also ignored the fact that she apparently was not going to be calling him Liam anymore. Damn it all, how had he screwed this up so fast?

Alex was surprisingly quiet, for which he was grateful. It was still hard to look at the werewolf and not think it was some costume and special effects make-up. Particularly now. He shivered to think of life stuck between two forms, forever a monster. A cold sweat broke out on his back.

He slowed again as they came to the end of the one-way street. "Where to?"

"Give me a second."

Watching her out the corner of his eye, he could admire the shape of her face, the intensity in her eyes. She was a woman worth fighting for, but he was fucking terrified of what was happening to him.

Staring out into the dark night, she said, "He's straight ahead of us."

All that was in front of them was a neon sign, half of the words missing. It should have been blinking 'Blitz and Blue Tattoos.' As it was, it said, 'Bli . . . nd B. . . at . . . s.'

"Blind Bats. Not great advertising," O'Shea said, pulling the SUV over to the curb. He didn't need to ask Rylee if she was sure. He knew her well enough to know better than to waste time.

"Blind Bats is a Troll species, probably the best kind of code they could come up with. Trolls aren't known for being particularly smart, or subtle." She slipped a few more weapons into her jacket.

"Anything I should know before we go in?" He unbuckled his seatbelt.

There was silence for a moment, and then she leaned forward so her face was only inches from his. The swirl of her tri-colored eyes hypnotized him, drew him in even closer.

Her lips were moving, and he tried to put the words together. "You aren't going to try and stop me? You aren't going to go bananas if I use the illusion of sex to make them drop their guard?"

"I can't promise you that. But I will try . . . ." He was unable to stop his traitorous hand from tucking a strand of auburn hair behind one of her ears. "Best thing I can do is go in there with you and keep you alive."

Alex butted his head between them. "Me tooooooooo!" His howl echoed in the car and they shushed him.

O'Shea put his hands up, "Yes, you can keep her safe too!"

The werewolf snorted and bobbed his head. "Yuppy doody, damn it."

Laughter spilled out of Rylee and O'Shea shook his head. Damn, she was beautiful, inside and out.

He frowned. "I do need one thing from you, before we go in."

"What?" Her eyes were sharp as they assessed him. What had made him think he'd be able to keep a secret from her? But he had to try. Because if she knew what he suspected he was turning into, whatever they had might be over before it even began.

O'Shea looked far too serious, though I suppose he was probably worried about fighting a school of

Trolls. Yes, like fish. His eyes seemed to darken even more, if that was possible, then he leaned over and planted his lips on mine, stealing any thoughts I would have of pulling back with his hand on the back of my neck.

The kiss was hot, like he'd lit a match inside of me next to a canteen of diesel fuel. I grabbed a hold of him, tasting his lips, fingers digging into his hair. I think he groaned, but I can't be sure it wasn't me.

Finally, after what was only moments but felt like an hour, I pulled back, my skin flushed through and through.

O'Shea's eyes were dazed and Alex was grumbling, muttering about stupid kissing boss man.

"Come on," the agent said, stepping out of the SUV. "Let's go."

I cleared my throat, and lightly touched my lips. What the hell? My blood was pounding, not unpleasantly, as I started out after him. I suppose if one was going to kick the bucket, one last kiss was in order.

Walking toward the tattoo shop, I checked my weapons, fingertips brushing against sword butts and my whip handle. Focusing on the kid, I let my Tracking ability guide me to where Ricky lay unconscious. More than that, I blocked what my head was already deeming 'O'Shea's Magic Kisses', as if he were a delectable concoction from the local bakery. Shit.

I was flushed with warmth and I strode toward the front door of the shop. There were no lights on inside. Alex romped and played in the snow beside me, burying his face and then lifting his head so I could see only his eyes.

"This is serious, no playing now," I said, and pulled one sword out from my back sheath. The copper and silver handle was cool against my skin. O'Shea slipped up beside me.

"Through the back?"

I nodded and we sidled our way around the building, sticking close to the old brick wall that caught at our clothes like scrubby little fingernails. Alex sort of listened. Beside us, he did an army crawl, but his ass and tail were sticking straight up in the air like a flag.

O'Shea lifted an eyebrow, and I shrugged. What could I say? Nothing would ever change the werewolf from what he was. Literally.

We reached the back door with no problems. I put my hand on it, turning the knob, but didn't open the door. It was unlocked. Sloppy work, but not surprising; I mean, shit, it was a Troll, not a freaking witch or Shaman.

O'Shea leaned close to me. "What can we expect, going in?"

Rolling my shoulders, I took a deep breath, the heat from his kiss still singing in my veins. "He'll try to use the kid against us."

"And?"

"We'll probably have to put our weapons down and do this bare-handed. And there will be more than just the one-eyed asshole." I was already seeing the fight in my head, trying to work out the best way to tackle the creep. It could be done.

"O'Shea," he looked over at me.

"Trolls, are tough, as in fighting even when their asses are on fire, but are stupid as a supernatural come."

"So kill 'em fast?"

"You got it."

Alex, ass still straight up in the air, sniffed the bottom of the door, lips rippling back over his teeth. His hackles rose, the hair along his spine standing straight up and a low growl beginning in the back of his throat.

I put a hand on his shoulders. "Easy, buddy."

"Bad Troll." He snapped out, teeth chattering. "No more meanie."

O'Shea shifted his weight. "In or out, we've got to move."

He was right.

"Alex, go back and knock on the front door. Hard. Then run back here. Got it?"

He sat up on his haunches, gave me a salute and galloped off, feet skidding in the snow as he rounded the corner.

Making eye contact with O'Shea, I didn't have to tell him anything. We heard the reverberation of Alex's knocking on the door; waiting ten seconds, we then opened the door and slid into the dim interior of the back room. Dirty linoleum floor, paint peeling off the walls, one flickering bulb overhead. Damn, it was like we'd walked into a true-to-life horror flick. The back room fed into a middle section that looked like a divider between renovations—un-sanded rough-hewn plywood—bled into the front portion of the shop, which was tiled and somewhat clean. At least, compared to the rest of the place.

O'Shea took the right side. I took the left; both of us with weapons out—swords to be exact. I slid along the wall, listening for the sound of a child. I could feel Ricky in my head, the thrum of his life strong and steady. He was still unconscious, a blessing if I—we—could get him out of here before he woke up. The scent of bleach wafted past my nose and then the scent of shit. Damn. I turned my head just enough to see O'Shea frown, his nose wrinkling.

Within moments, we'd made our way to the front of the tattoo parlour, checking every crevice, but the place was empty.

I stood in the center of the room, breathing shallowly. Gods be damned, this place reeked of Trolls. My head spun. Trolls. Shit, if there really *was* more than one, we were going to have a bloody mess on our hands. Again, I wished we had run the bastard through when we'd dumped him on the side of the road. He'd deserved it—he'd killed a cop—but we'd been in a hurry. A terrible excuse for what was becoming a mistake that could cost more lives.

The soft click of nails on the linoleum brought my head around. Alex was tiptoeing in, his nose wrinkled up as I wished I could do too, to block the smell.

"Fuck, this shit is stinky." He waved a claw in front of his nose.

O'Shea's eyebrows climbed. "I think that's the most complete sentence I've ever heard him say."

Ignoring them both, I *reached* for Ricky, let my senses trace him. Eyes half-closed, I followed the feel of him to the middle section, the piece that hadn't been finished. Standing over it, I laid my hands on the wood, felt the thrum of energy still there. A minor spell, one so small you wouldn't notice it unless you were looking hard. A spell that disrupted under my touch, my Immunity pulling it apart. Blind Bat Trolls didn't carry magic; they had to be getting help from someone else. We were in trouble.

I waved Alex closer. "Can you fit your claws into the edge here?" There was a small lip on the joint between the two walls, invisible until you slid your hand over it. Alex sniffed it, slid his claws along the edge, working them until they were underneath. With a violent jerk, he yanked the whole panel off with a shriek of wood and splinters bursting out everywhere.

O'Shea went to the opening first. "Are we crossing the Veil?"

"No, this was hidden by a small spell. Nothing major." The opening was dark and barely wide enough for a Troll's body, but there was plenty of room for us. I led the way, blade in front of me.

The flick of a light behind me spun me around. I clamped my hand over the flashlight O'Shea had produced, keeping my voice as low as I could. "No light."

His voice was controlled, but I could hear the anger in it. "We can't help him if we break our necks."

"We can't help him if we get caught before we get to him," I said, peering ahead into the dim interior.

"You don't think they heard the werewolf ripping off their front door?"

I snatched the flashlight from him, jammed it in my pocket. *Thinks he knows everything. Stupid man.* I didn't want to admit he was probably right.

Of course, timing was everything. There was a roar from behind us, and what light we had from the murky shop was blocked by a Troll's body as he squeezed into the opening we'd just passed through.

I flicked the flashlight on and pointed it straight at the beast's eyes, shocking it with the sudden light. The Troll—its flapping, greasy puke-green skin shaking with anger—roared again, reaching blindly for us, eyes averted.

"You're up," I yelled at O'Shea.

The agent spun, slicing through the Troll's belly, dodging the flailing hands with ease. Troll guts spilled out onto the ground, neon-blue and green, the blood a pale orange that glowed under the light. The beast groaned, grabbing at its stomach in vain.

"The boy is dead," he spluttered out, dropping to his knees, blood dripping from his grinning lips. O'Shea didn't waste any more time. A second slice of his blade and the Troll's head rolled from his shoulders, face stuck in a macabre grin.

"Okay, lights on, let's go," I said.

"He lied?"

"Yes, they always lie." Okay, maybe not always, but for the most part, Trolls were liars.

But, like every rule, there was an exception. One big fucking, messed up exception.

18

We wove our way through the timbers of the building, the path obvious with the stink and Troll shit littering the way. Alex did his best to avoid stepping in it, as did we, but the stinking piles were everywhere, smeared like they'd been skating in it for fun. Disgusting creatures.

It took us ten minutes to make our way through the building before we were faced with a decision. The pathway branched, one taking us to the right, the other taking us to a hole in the ground that was surrounded with bones, shit, and a flapping material that looked like an old, partially shredded bedsheet.

"Let me guess, the hole," O'Shea asked, though it wasn't really a question. Ricky was close, and when I leaned over the hole, the sensation of being right on top of him was overwhelming.

"You guessed it," I muttered. "Why is it always the nasty places? Just once, I'd like to end up finding a kid somewhere clean, somewhere not covered in shit or blood."

The three of us peered down into the darkness. I handed the flashlight back to O'Shea. "Here."

He shone the light from his side. "Nothing, I can't see anything. It's as if something is swallowing the light."

Oh, that was far too perceptive and he didn't even know what he was saying. There was one species of Trolls that was worse than the others, and so rare I hadn't even considered the possibility of running into one. Lighteaters. And they had some ability with magic. That explained the spell on the entranceway. To top it off, they were smart little bastards, not as big as their counterparts, but their brains made up for their lack of size. Son of a bitch, we were in for a fight.

The flashlight took that moment to blink off; I raised my sword. "Back away from the hole."

I heard O'Shea shuffle back in the darkness, Alex stayed all but glued to my side.

Licking my lips, the foul air coated my tongue. "We have a big bad coming out of that hole, and we can't fight it in the dark. We have to get back to the shop, now."

"Alex sees."

"You lead the way, buddy," I said. But I made the call too late—our luck wasn't going to hold. A blast of air erupted from the hole, sending us tumbling backwards into the framing of the building.

My right leg smashed across a piece of a two-by-four, I'm guessing by the feel, stopping my flight through the air and slamming me to the ground.

A slobber-filled voice called out to us. "So, you've come for the boy? I've wanted to meet you for a long time, Tracker. You have quite the reputation. It's too late, the boy is dead."

The thing was, I could feel him, feel the pulse of his heart as if it were my own, so I knew the Lighteater was lying. "Liar, liar, pants on fire," I said, using the framework to pull myself to my feet. My leg wasn't broken, but I had a serious Charlie horse, the muscles cramping hard enough to keep me from putting any weight on it.

The Lighteater laughed, its breath filling the air with the rot of swamps, a manure pile that had dead things buried in it.

I didn't want to hit O'Shea or Alex, the darkness making us as deadly to each other as to anything we might try and fight.

"Come here, Tracker, I want to see if you are as . . . delicious . . . as reputed."

"Why don't you just get on with it then," I said, half-hopping to one side, keeping one hand out to feel for the framing of the house, the other hand holding my sword at the ready.

"I like to play games. Don't you? Playing with your food is so much more fun than just eating it." The Lighteater purred, and then smacked its lips, the click of teeth like nails on a chalkboard.

"Adamson?" O'Shea called out.

"Stay there! And stay down. He wants me, so he's going to get me." The thing was, in a tight, dark space like this, I could end up killing O'Shea or Alex if I wasn't careful, and I had no doubt the Lighteater would be all over that possibility.

There was only one thing I could do. I Tracked O'Shea and Alex, holding the threads of their lives inside my head. While I couldn't see them, I could feel where they were. The double rush of emotions dropped me to my knees, and I struggled to get a hold on them. I'd never tried Tracking multiple people in this close of a proximity all at the same time, and I was about to add a third. I reached for the Lighteater's life threads, grabbing hold of them with a vengeance. Now I could 'see' him too.

Gotcha, ya stupid bastard.

I slid sideways. "Stay down, O'Shea. I've got this one."

"Make it quick, Adamson."

Yup, that was the plan.

The Lighteater laughed, and I closed my eyes. I couldn't see anyway. I backed away from the Troll, the hole where other Trolls likely waited, and my partners.

Feeling my way, I hobbled backwards, doing my best not to stumble. The Lighteater followed me, the pulse of his energy getting incrementally closer. A piece of frame seemed to reach up and yank my feet out from under me, landing me hard on my back, the wind knocked out of me.

Ah, fuck, here he comes.

The Lighteater rushed me and I swung upward with my sword. I could feel his surprise, felt a sudden burst of fear.

"Oooh, you didn't know I could do that, did ya?" I gloated, rolling to my knees. He hung back, the pulse of his life thumping steady and strong. I was about to change that.

I swung hard and fast, anticipating the thump of flesh and bone, the reverberation up through my blade and into my arm. Reverberation, yes, flesh and bone, not so much.

My blade bit deep into a piece of the building's framework, nearly severing it.

"FUCK!" I yanked hard, pulling the blade free, just in time to get slammed to the ground by the Lighteater, his mouth, teeth, and rotting breath mere inches from my face. I flung my body to the side, throwing us both into more wooden framing, the crack and groan of the structure more than a little alarming, but that wasn't what was going to eat me.

"Stupid bitch, you'll bring the place down on us," he snarled, clawed hands digging into my shoulders as he slammed my upper body into the ground. Several times.

I grit my teeth and jammed my left leg between us, shoving him up enough to loosen his grip on my shoulders. He snarled and snot—or maybe it was drool, I couldn't tell the difference in the dark—plopped onto my face, slid down my neck. It smelled of vomit.

We rolled again, and I reached for my backup sword, swinging it out and around. The Lighteater raised his hand to me and a bar of light sprung out of his fingertips, a spell to fry me to a cinder. The brilliant white bar lit the darkness up and gave me my first glimpse of the Troll, a split second of black and gray skin that looked to be sloughing off, huge cat's eyes wide with glee. Then the spell hit my sword, raced down the blade and fizzled as it touched my skin, leaving us once more in the dark.

"You are an Immune?" He gurgled, his fear heavy in the back of my head.

"Surprise!" I brought my sword down, straight through his heart. There was no last cry for mercy, no cry for help.

But I hadn't let go of his life force, and this close, his death hit me like a runaway train. I tumbled backwards, felt his memories and desires wash over me. There was light and dark in him, mostly dark, but the light . . . it was the memories of pain and a lost love that had gone before him that struck me down, of being cast out from the other Trolls, being alone and wishing for a friend. Those emotions faded, slowly dissipated, and finally I was alone in my head with Alex and O'Shea, both of whom I let go of, so I could get a hold of my own feelings.

"Adamson?"

"I'm here. Try your flashlight. It should work now that he's dead." I sat there, shaking. Trolls, no one had ever said they had much to offer the world, and yet in the Lighteater's death, I'd seen how much he'd wanted to do, though he'd known it would never be. Heavy, it was too heavy for me to deal with right now. I didn't have any desire to feel bad for a supernatural that kidnapped children, raped women, and in general was a destructive form of chaos for nothing other than its own pleasure.

Trembling, I got to my feet as O'Shea flicked on the flashlight. Shading my eyes, I limped my way over to him and Alex, picking my feet up carefully as I traversed the broken framework.

Leaping toward me, Alex wrapped himself around my legs, almost taking me down to the floor again. I patted him on the head, "Okay, let's get going."

"You think there are more Trolls?" O'Shea asked.

"At least our friend we left behind, but probably not too many more. They don't do well in large numbers for long periods of time; they can turn cannibalistic at the drop of a hat," I said as I tried to get the worst of the—drool, snot, whatever it was—off me.

O'Shea said nothing, just flicked the light over the hole. "I can see a ladder, and a rough wall. You think it's safe to go down now?"

I shrugged and leaned over the hole. "Safe as it's ever going to be, I think."

In the end, we left Alex to guard the topside. Not only could he give us a heads up if someone else was coming our way, he could see in the dark.

The ladder we climbed down was rickety, the wood creaking under our weight. How the hell had the Trolls used it without crushing it?

O'Shea asked that very question, giving me the opportunity to look smart. Or maybe, not so much.

"I don't know." *Clever girl, he's sure to be impressed!* I ignored my inner snark, and checked out the area we were standing in. "Probably this wasn't a Troll hole to begin with. They are good jumpers and climbers, probably didn't ever use the ladder. Likely is, they put it up just for us."

"So we could be dealing with another kind of supernatural too, whatever created this place first?"

Gods help us, I hoped not. "Probably not, the Trolls would have cleaned out the area before settling in."

I pushed some dirt with my boot, reached for Ricky and froze. His heartbeat was gone. It wasn't like with the Lighteater where I felt him die, he was just . . . gone. Snuffed out like a candle.

"Oh, shit!" Was the kid's life somehow tied to the Lighteaters?

Latching onto what was left of Ricky's still threads, I ran toward him, O'Shea right with me.

"The kid?"

"Yes."

Thank the gods he was not a man who needed every freaking detail explained to him.

We ran through the dark, dirt tunnel, flashlight bobbing hard. Downward we ran, the angle of the ground getting steeper and steeper until it suddenly flattened out and we could see again. We were standing in what looked like a replica of the tattoo shop up above.

Sitting in a client's chair, the Troll we should have killed on the last salvage lounged, a long lanky child crumpled at his feet. The Troll's mottled skin drooped heavily, and his singular eye glared at us behind what looked like a glass covering to protect it. The shine of metal strapping the glass to his head showed a patched together piece of equipment that would, to a degree, keep his eye safe. Orange and yellow flapping skin seemed to wave at us as he moved, and he let out a long wet fart splattering the back of his chair. Fucking disgusting. He smiled, lips drooping, broken and crooked teeth glittering at me.

"Well, it looks as if you were too late to save the brat. Stupid, Tracker. You didn't really think I'd let you get close enough to kill me and save the kid, did you?"

I wanted to rush him, slice him up, and serve him to the fishes in small, bite-sized pieces, and if I had my way, before the day was done, that's exactly what was going to happen.

"Stupid. The Lighteater gave the brat a fake heart beat. And you fell for it."

Ricky was gone, his threads to this world cut before I could get to him, a perfect bait to draw me in. And the Troll's plan had worked. Maybe I'd been under-estimating Trolls; maybe they were smarter than I'd been giving them credit for.

He stood, his two-pronged dick starting to get a hard on, stretched and flipped me off. "Come get me, if you dare."

Challenging the Tracker you'd just told you'd fooled, egging her on to come at you? Nope, still dumb as dirt.

O'Shea circled to the left and I circled to the right.

The Troll backed up a step. "That's not fair; you can't go two at a time."

"I'm not interested in fair," I said, my anger raging to the surface. As with every case I took on, it felt, in a way, like Berget's case all over again. It was my fault this kid was snatched, my fault he was dead. Guilt flamed the anger into a boiling rage that exploded in a flurry of movement. I closed on the Troll, blade singing through the air. He backed up and right into O'Shea, who took the Troll's right arm off with a single downward slice.

Screaming, he fell to his knees, sobbing and plead-ing, his one arm flopping on the ground like a fish out of water, the stump where it had been scabbing over in less than a second. I stepped forward to finish him off when he launched from the ground, teeth snapping at my face, claws digging into my shoulder. My hand went numb and I dropped my sword. With his powerful hand he could easily snap my arm, even rip it off and leave me to bleed out.

I shoved my free hand under the glass and metal cage covering his remaining eye, my fingers digging in around the soft orb. Voice as calm as I could make it under the circumstances, I said, "Let me go, or I'll take this one too."

The Troll froze, his teeth digging through several layers of skin.

"I'll let you go, if you take your hands off me. Otherwise, you'll lose the eye, you bastard," I said.

O'Shea stood just back from us, sword raised and pointed at the base of the Troll's neck. "Don't," I said. "I will make the deal with him. Just trust me."

The agent's jaw twitched and he slowly lowered his sword.

"Let go of my arm, and then I'll let go of your eye. Deal?"

He grunted, which I took for a yes. As he removed his claws from around my shoulder, we stood up together, my fingers still dug in around his eye.

"Let it go now; you promised," he whined, his free hand resting against my arm. There was no way he'd push me, even he wasn't that much of a dumbass.

I squeezed the orb and yanked, ripping it from its socket. "I lied, you piece of shit."

The Troll wailed and writhed, flailing about, his screams echoing off the walls of the 'shop.'

When I moved to finish him, O'Shea blocked me. "Wait, I want to ask him a question."

Snorting, I backed up a step, waving for the agent to go ahead. Either way, the Troll was going to die. Ricky was gone; there was no other amends I could make, except to kill his killer.

So what punishment will you receive, for taking so long, for being a party to the kid's death? Guilt rolled in me, making me weak with its truth.

"Why did you really take the kid?"

I made a move as if to answer. We already knew this.

"Fuck you, human," the Troll screamed, a mixture of clear liquid and orange blood dripping from between his fingers.

Again, O'Shea pressed him. "No, this is more than just you going after the Tracker."

Whimpering, the Troll crouched on the ground, his sniffles pitiful. "I can't tell you."

My jaw dropped. What the hell?

"You are going to die, either way," O'Shea said, running the tip of his sword across the Trolls remaining arm. The stump of his other arm vibrated with each pump of his seven-valve heart, faster with each swipe of O'Shea's blade.

"Tell me," the agent said, "And I'll make it clean." Wrong thing to say to a Troll, but O'Shea couldn't know that.

With a roar, the Troll threw himself at O'Shea, taking the agent's sword deep into his chest, but not through his heart. They tumbled to the ground, O'Shea underneath; the Troll rearing his head back for a strike that would sever O'Shea's head.

I didn't even think about whether or not what I was doing was wrong. My sword flashed in the dim light as I whipped it forward, taking the Troll's head, silencing him permanently. With a thump, his floppy-skinned head hit the floor, tongue hanging out, sightless holes staring up into nothing.

O'Shea lay on his back for another second. "Thanks."

"Yeah, anytime." The image of O'Shea under the Troll unsettled me.

"I'm okay."

I stared at him. "I know."

"Then why do you look like you're going to cry?" His own eyes had a soft glimmer to them, as if he was affected by how I was feeling. Which it couldn't be, because although we'd slept together, I wasn't altogether sure he felt anything but lust for me. Whereas I knew I was falling hard for the bloody agent. Damn, I was no good at this.

I turned away from him, unsettled by seeing my own emotions reflected on his face. I made my way to Ricky's side, dropped to my knees beside him, and put my hands on his chest. In a last ditch effort, hoping my ability to Track had failed me, I pressed hard, whispered a prayer to anyone who would listen. He was already cold, but I'd known he would be before I ever put a hand to him. The threads of his life had been cut and there was no coming back for Ricky.

Nothing, there was nothing.

I leaned back on my heels and tipped my head back.

O'Shea stepped up beside me then crouched down, his shoulder brushing against mine. "Even you can't save them all."

"He died because I made a mistake. Died because I couldn't get to him in time, because I put myself first." I shoved the agent, sending him sprawling on the ground. Standing up, I looked around for something to wrap the kid in, something to pack him out in.

"It isn't your fault, Adamson. They faked it; the kid wasn't even alive."

I went to shove him again, anger and pain all wrapped up inside me, desperate for release. The tinkle of rocks under foot stopped me. I held a finger up and touched my ear. O'Shea went silent and we listened.

There was nothing else, or at least, I couldn't hear anything.

"More Trolls," O'Shea said with a confidence that surprised me.

"I didn't hear—"

He grabbed my arm. "Trust me," he said, his face grim as he pulled me along. "There's more Trolls, and they're hungry."

19

couldn't leave without Ricky. It was the least I could do, returning him to his mother. He was light, maybe a hundred pounds, but it was a dead weight. O'Shea slung him over his shoulder like it was nothing, surprising me, and we ran for the ladder.

Behind us, the noises grew louder, and then a roar of angry voices permeated the air. The scent of Troll shit and fermenting meat grew stronger. It didn't matter which end of a Troll you had to deal with, it was vile.

I hoped they'd stop for a snack on their buddy. Maybe they would decide to eat him before coming after us. Gruesome, but it would give us the time we needed.

Pushing O'Shea ahead of me, I guarded the bottom of the ladder while the agent climbed with his awkward load. "I'm up." He called down, and I started up the ladder, feet and hands scrabbling at the rungs.

Hot breath swirled around me and I dared a look down. Four Trolls below me, staring up with their beady, somewhat sagging eyes. "Light!" O'Shea flashed the beam down. Swearing and cursing floated up around me along with their nasty breath, and I rushed up the last few rungs. "Go, go, go!"

Alex bolted ahead of us, and O'Shea's light bobbed crazily, but we made it out of the shop to the SUV without any problem.

Flinging open the side door and reaching for my black box, I grabbed one of Milly's spell bombs and cracked it open. Spinning on my heel, I cocked my arm like a shot putter, and threw it hard at the shop, the ignition word falling from my lips.

"Incendio!"

The bomb hit the corner and exploded into flame that raced across the wooden timbers, even though they were wet. A whoosh of thick black smoke exploded out the front window, shards of glass spraying around us. I grabbed a second spell bomb in case the Trolls tried to make it past the flames. Apparently, they were going to play it smart for once. Carefully, I put the second spell bomb back into my black hard case and tucked it into my bag.

I stared at the tattoo parlor, smoke billowing out of it, flames licking up the sides and putting out the neon sign completely.

"We should go," I said, getting into the front seat.

O'Shea nodded, wrapping Ricky in a blue tarp and placing him in the very back of the SUV.

Alex bounced around us, giving yips of excitement, until his nose wrinkled and he poked at Ricky's body with a single claw. "Dead."

I didn't answer him; his nose was on the mark again. Alex curled up beside me, his feet and our shoes and clothes reeking of Troll shit.

"We've got to get cleaned up before we take Ricky to his mom," O'Shea said.

I didn't argue, he was right and I didn't have the strength to do anything more than nod.

The fact that Adamson was silent on their drive away from the Trolls concerned O'Shea, but he put it aside and stepped on the gas. The faster he got them cleaned up and Ricky taken home, the faster he could deal with whatever plagued his body. Rage and hunger roared within him, and it was all he could do to keep it under control. And it wasn't just hunger of the belly, either. The scent of Rylee's hair and skin made him hard, even with the overlying scent of Troll. All of which he didn't like thinking about because he shouldn't have been able to smell any of it. He might be able to function, dealing with the supernatural as it was thrown at him, but with his own senses kicking into overdrive, his grasp on reality was slipping.

Traversing the icy, nearly abandoned, snow-covered roads, he made his way to his home. It was in the middle of a family-type subdivision, the yards all immaculate, though under the snow it was hard to tell. He pulled into the driveway and hit the automatic door opener for the garage. Nothing happened.

"Sorry," Adamson said, "That'll be me and Alex causing problems."

Of course, he'd forgotten about that. Then again, it might be him too, now. Fear stabbed through him. God, to think he could be a supernatural now . . . he pushed the thought away, though he'd already seen enough evidence staring him in the face that he knew he was just putting off the inevitable.

He glanced in the back. Alex stared at the ceiling, but Adamson was awake, her eyes watching him. He had a moment of insight, seeing the wariness there, the uncertainty, the lack of trust. In that moment, he could see that she was, in her own way, as much as a wild creature as Alex. It hurt, knowing that for a moment or two, he'd had more than her trust; he suspected he'd held her heart too. What a clusterfuck this was.

"Come on, we can get cleaned up here and then we can take my truck."

"What about Alex?" Adamson untangled herself from the werewolf slowly.

"He can come in, but can you hide him?" O'Shea pointed out at the bright lights on either side of his dark house, a face peering out each window. The neighbourhood thought they were a freaking watch when it came to his comings and goings. There was no way they'd miss a werewolf playing in the snow.

She was already nodding, auburn hair shifting around her face, hands reaching forward. "Pass me my bag."

He flipped the bag back to her. "Here."

She slid out a collar studded in diamonds and buckled it onto Alex. The werewolf's image wavered, and for a brief second all O'Shea saw was a big black dog of indiscriminate breeding. Another blink and Alex in all his werewolf glory was back.

Adamson shivered and started for the door; O'Shea got out and went around the side to meet her. It was hard to think no one would notice the two hundred pound werewolf, but again, he had to trust her. He did trust her. And that in itself was a bloody freaking miracle. Not that he had to, but that he did. Which was going to make what he had to do so much harder.

"Rylee, you need to look at this." O'Shea's voice was soft, his tone far more sympathetic than I'd ever heard him before. We were giving Ricky a final once over, making sure any wounds weren't gaping and obvious before we went inside to clean ourselves up.

My mind circled around a single truth, one I couldn't escape. The Troll would never have killed Ricky if I'd taken care of things, if I'd done what I should have in the beginning.

"What now?"

"The Troll didn't kill him."

My hands on the boys clothing stilled and I stared at O'Shea. "How do you know that?"

"Multiple bullet wounds. And the kid has been dead just a few hours." He pointed at a wound on Ricky's back. "That is far too decomposed. This kid has been dead for two weeks at least. Probably killed the night he went missing."

Bullet wounds, dead longer, for at least two weeks. He was right; it couldn't have been the Troll.

O'Shea stood and moved around the body, every inch of him an agent in that moment. "My best guess is the Troll grabbed the kid's body after he'd been shot and killed; it would be simpler to keep a kid quiet that's dead, than alive. Wouldn't matter if he forgot to feed him, or if he had to leave for an extended period of time. Of course, there is also the fact that he, your Troll friend there, knew how you'd react if you found a dead body, rather than a live kid. Psychological warfare in a way."

I closed my eyes, let the relief flow out of me, followed by a sharp burst of fear. I should have thanked O'Shea, should have been grateful. And I was, but I couldn't say it. Either way, the kid was gone and I was going to have to tell his mother. Regardless, the ending was the same for her. To know that the Lighteater could so easily fake Ricky's life, to emulate it enough that I fell into their trap; that had my nerves dancing. If I couldn't trust my own ability to Track . . . what then? I swallowed hard, pushing my fears aside. I wished there was someone who knew more than me, someone who I could turn to, to ask. But there wasn't. So for now, I would have to just suck it up. No different than usual.

"Let's get him wrapped up tight. I don't want anything left to chance." We worked quickly, tying the body up, removing all traces of our own fingerprints and hairs with a simple spell of Milly's.

"*Abradant*," I whispered, igniting the spell. A soft pink glow flowed over the boy's body. "That'll keep the detectives in the dark."

O'Shea said nothing, closing the back of the SUV, then headed into the house, the snow and dark muffling his footsteps.

I followed O'Shea into the one story rancher, typical of the new building style in the area. I kept my fingers jammed in my pockets and Alex stayed tight to my side. Even with the cold air and the wind, I could smell the Troll shit on us. Damn, it was bad stuff and already hardening on our clothes.

O'Shea went in first, lights bloomed, and we followed. Shutting the door behind us, I couldn't help but stare. We were standing in the kitchen, black and white decor with a splash of blue here and there. Damn, either he had an interior designer or the man had some taste. Stainless steel appliances, granite countertops, and clean—everything was freaking spotless. That didn't surprise me though; O'Shea was particular about everything he did.

I was shaking, not with cold, but the adrenaline let down, my fingers tight around Alex's collar as I kept him close to my side.

"Nice joint," I said, meaning it.

O'Shea slipped out of his coat and shoes, threw them into a room off the kitchen, what looked like the mudroom, then he continued to peel out of his clothes, much to my, I'll admit, pleasure. He lifted his eyes to me.

"Strip."

"Oh no, I'm enjoying this just fine. I don't need to join you." I couldn't stop the smile from slipping across my lips. Yes indeed, I might have told myself no more touching, but I could still look. *Damn*! A very large part of me wanted to rescind my previous vow not to let him affect or touch me.

"You smell like Troll shit and I'm not going to take you to the kid's mother with that stench in my truck."

Bugger, he had a point. Letting go of Alex's collar, I shrugged out of my coat, noting a large chunk of mung on one shoulder. Damn it that was nasty. Amazing though how quickly I got used to it. Within seconds, I was down to my bra and panties (thank the gods they were at least matching), and my clothes were handed off to O'Shea. Third time in less than two days I was down to my skin and a few scraps of material between me, O'Shea, and full nudity. Of course, the last time was much more fun. *Stop it!*

O'Shea strode past me, and I stepped back to keep from touching his bare skin. "Stay here, I'll get you something to wear," he said, walking deeper into the house.

My eyes tracked him, his body hard and muscled, and his shorts not leaving a lot to my imagination. Not that I needed imagination to visualize what was under them. I closed my eyes. *Think about other things, Rylee. Think about how you are going to explain to Jewel you messed up, how to explain to O'Shea you can't be his partner . . .*

Faris.

His name reverberated through me as if someone had spoken it. My eyes flew open and I stared around me, my weapons piled on the kitchen table. I grabbed my sword, my fingers gripping the handle.

Licking my lips, I moved slowly, both from the cold and a desire for stealth. Alex was sitting beside me, eyebrows lifted high.

"What do you smell, buddy?" I asked, my voice pitched low.

Lifting his nose, he scented the air, tongue held tight between his front teeth, just the pink tip visible against his black fur.

"Bacon."

That was not what I'd expected. "Nothing else?"

Snuffling the air, he swiveled on his haunches as O'Shea came back into the room a thick green robe slung over his arm. "What is it?"

"Smelling," Alex said, taking in a lungful of air. "Man with gun. Boss."

I patted him on the head and laid my sword on the table. "Okay, thanks." For now I would chalk it up to being tired, cold, and sore.

O'Shea tossed me the robe and I slipped it on, groaning as the cool air was blocked from my skin and the soft fleece enveloped me. His cologne clung to the material, the musk a heady drug to me. I could breathe it in all night and not get tired of the scent.

I opened my eyes to see O'Shea staring at me, his eyes dilated, nostrils flaring. "I'll get Alex cleaned up," he said, but his eyes said other things. Things my own pulse began to echo.

He disappeared into the mudroom, then came back and grabbed Alex. "Come on, let's get that shit off your feet."

Alex went with him, tail drooping and a grumble under his breath. I gave him a wave and a smile, grateful that O'Shea was willing to help out with Alex. I moved deeper into the house, burying my bare toes into the lush carpet of the living room. The floor was warm; it had to be in-floor heating, which was a nice perk.

The main living area was as tastefully decorated as the kitchen, the colors shifting into rich hues of mahogany and cream with one wall covered in a painted scene taking up the whole thing. I moved closer to the painting. A lone tree painted with broken and gnarled branches, it was nearly sheared through the middle, either by fire or ax, I couldn't tell. Leaves scattered on the ground and the moon—glimpsed between scattered clouds—were the main focal points, besides the tree itself. But the longer I looked, the more I saw. Bats, an owl hidden in the branches, even shoots of new life peeking out through the fallen leaves, the distant silhouette of a wolf. A wave of nostalgia rose within me, a desire for something more than what I had with my life. For some reason the painting made me think of my lack of family, about how my life was never really my own. Not that I would have it any other way.

"You like it?" O'Shea said from behind me. I let out a slow breath, breathed in the scent of wet dog.

I stalled. "Did Alex behave?"

"Yes, I left him in the mudroom to dry off some," he leaned closer. "The painting, do you like it?"

Why did it matter? So I shrugged. "Yeah, it's okay." I sure as shit wasn't going to tell him about the emotions it evoked. I shifted on my feet, uncertain where this was going, if anywhere. I was in his house and I was uncomfortable.

His hands settled on my shoulders, "I'm sorry for screwing things up. I know that I could have handled it better."

He was apologizing? Very slowly I relaxed into his arms as he pulled me tight against his chest.

"I don't do secrets. And I don't do possessive jealousy," I said, my fingers finding the edges of his hands.

"I'm not keeping secrets, I just . . ." he paused, seeming to gather his thoughts. "I'm just struggling with this world you've shown me. It doesn't follow the rules I understand."

Very gently, he kissed the side of my neck. "Rylee, please, give me a second chance."

I melted against him, his voice and the emotion in it undoing whatever resolve I'd had. "Damn it." I turned in his arms, our lips seeking each other out. With him, I was weak, could feel the desire crush my conviction that being right was better.

Lifting me up in his arms, he walked us to the bathroom. A two-person shower inlaid with gray and white river rock beckoned and we obliged. He scrubbed my back and I scrubbed his, our hands pausing to caress and touch, our lips following suit. Underneath it all, the pain of losing Ricky rose up in me, Liam's hands soothing the path for the tears that were soon falling. The steady stream of hot water, his body shaped around mine, he kissed away the pain. Guilt, my nearly constant companion, rode me hard, whispered to me that I would never wash it away, no matter how much I tried. Berget's death would always be on my shoulders, and with each subsequent child I lost, I pulled further away from redeeming her death.

"You can't save them all."

He was right, and I let out a deep, hiccupping sigh. No point in agreeing, but my heart still wanted to believe I could save them all. So I changed the subject.

"You know how many people see me cry?" I hid my face under the hot water.

"I'm betting less than you can count on two fingers."

A ruthful chuckle escaped me, and I moved as if to step out of the shower.

Liam's hands stopped me, settling into the crook of my waist. "Come here."

With a gentle pull, he brought me back to him, the hot water sluicing around us as he picked me up and settled me on his hips. Like I weighed nothing; not that I'm a beefy girl, but damn.

His skin was hot against mine, hot and slick with water and soap.

Curling my legs around him, I held him tight, as he pressed my back against the cool tiles and plunged into me. My gasp turned into a groan as his hips pumped, bringing me to a climax with an ease and speed that was a little frightening. In some ways he knew my body better than I did. Holding me against the tile with his body, our breathing harsh in the confines of the stall, his hands traced down to mine, our fingers tangling. Dark eyes met mine, an emotion flitting through them I rarely saw. "I didn't hurt you did I?"

I was surprised he would even ask. "No, I'm hardly a china doll."

Smiling, the worry in his eyes eased, shifting once more to desire. His lips found mine, the taste of his mouth a slice of heaven I couldn't seem to get enough of. In a matter of minutes we were back where we started, bodies surging toward one another. I would take every minute of this and the inevitable soreness that would come later. He was worth it and then some.

Finally, after much persuasion, Liam let me out of the shower, though he made one last attempt to drag me back in. Smiling, I sidestepped his hands and dried off before he could snatch me back to the heat of the water and his body. It was harder than it should have been to walk out of the bathroom. For the first time, I felt good after a salvage gone bad. Because of Liam. Shit, I was so falling for him. I smiled at the thought, not bothered by it as I would have been once. Wrapped in a thick, plush towel I made my way out to the living room.

Which was as we'd left it, with one snarling addition.

A low rumble filled the room. I turned my head to see Alex on all fours, back hunched, tail and fur stiff. Teeth bared, he continued to growl, his eyes locked on O'Shea who'd stepped up behind me.

Angry werewolf, small space, bad combination. I made a move as if to intersect, but O'Shea stopped me, putting me behind him.

"He can't keep acting like you are property. He's not the top dog here." Oh, for . . . would the gods ever show me some mercy and let me deal with minor egos for once?

"At this point, it doesn't matter. One bite and you'll be turning furry." That was if Alex didn't lose his shit and go mental. I really, really did not want to be forced to kill Alex. Just the thought made me choke up.

"Alex, settle down." I put myself back between the werewolf and O'Shea. "I mean it!"

But he didn't settle down. Quite the contrary. "No biting," he growled out, then leapt forward, knocking me behind him. I hit the floor, more shocked than anything, my towel slipping open. Alex grumbled his way over to me, casting dirty glances over his shoul-

der at O'Shea. With two claws, he pulled my towel
back up, covering me. "Rylee loves Alex."

I closed my eyes, and bowed my head. How was I
going to explain this one?

Alex gave a yelp, and then a baritone growl filled
the air. My eyes flew open, but my brain couldn't
quite make sense of what I was seeing.

O'Shea had Alex lifted off the floor by his neck,
and had pinned him against the wall. That was weird
enough on its own.

"Alex sorry!" The werewolf yelped, writhing hard
against O'Shea's hands. "Sorry! You Boss!"

His tail was tucked up through his legs and he
started to pee, urine dripping off his fur. I scrambled
to my feet, the low growl still rumbling in the room
. . . from . . . Liam?

I put a hand on his shoulder and he flinched as if I'd
hit him, turning dark eyes to me—dark eyes swirling
with flecks of gold. I kept my hand on his shoulder;
the last thing he needed was for me to pull away. Shit,
shit, shit! When had Alex bitten him? Or maybe it
wasn't Alex. I thought about Liam's hip—that was
the moment he'd started to seem off. Could he have
contracted something from the bear Guardian?

Carefully, knowing I was handling a very precarious
situation, I put pressure on his arm. "Let him down."

Liam let go and Alex hit the floor, cowering.

"Go dry off," I said, pointing back to the mudroom.
He was still damp and dripping on the carpet.

Scrabbling, tail tucked between his legs and head
down, Alex trotted back the way he'd come, nails
clicking on the tile floor.

"This is what you weren't sure of," I asked softly, still not taking my hand from him. Oh my God, he was going to shift on the next full moon, but into what? And would he be able to shift back? I started to shiver.

"You think I'm a monster," Liam said, stepping back from me.

I shook my head vehemently. "No!"

He took another step back. "I don't blame you."

"Liam, don't do this. Don't push me away. I was wrong before when I tried to put distance between us," I swallowed hard. "I'm not used to being with someone, and it scares me. But I don't want to lose you." I followed him, not letting him put the distance between us that he wanted to.

"I would have killed him if you hadn't stopped me," he roared. "I can feel this rage building in me, and I either want to kill something or . . ." His eyes raked over me. I shivered, not unpleasantly, with the thoughts of revisiting the shower.

I looked up at him. He was strong and good, and he had every reason to keep hating me. Yet he'd let it all go, every last grudge he'd had against me. Milly hadn't tempted him; he accepted I knew more than him, trusted me to lead. He'd cleaned Troll shit off my werewolf. There were not a lot of guys who could come even close to comparing to him. There was no way I was going to let go of him now.

"Liam, no matter what, this changes nothing between us. You won't be different, you will just be more. Stronger, faster, harder to kill. But you'll still be you. The rage is because you have a wolf trapped in you now that wants to get out. It's still you."

Reaching for him, I pulled back when he glared at me. "I don't want your pity."

I threw my hands into the air. "It isn't pity, you idiot! I love you."

The words hung between us, hovering with their weight. I swallowed hard, but held my ground.

We stood there, staring at each other until the soft clicking of Alex's nails drew my attention. The werewolf leaned against the doorjamb between the kitchen and the living room, eyes lowered, tail drooped. "Dry now." He swirled a front paw in a circle on the floor. "Rylee, we go now?"

I looked back at Liam, the glare on his face directed at Alex. He still hadn't responded to my somewhat un-romantic declaration of love, though I had no doubt he'd heard me.

"Yeah, we're going now. Go get my bag, Alex." The werewolf ducked his head and left us standing there, in an uneasy standoff.

"What are you going to tell Agent Valley?" Sure, I was welcome on the team, but the AA Division knew what I was, had always been. Liam becoming supernatural, well, that was likely a big no-no. But that was just a guess. By the look on his face, he'd come to the same conclusion.

"Nothing."

Alex came back in and tossed my bag at my feet. I yanked out my extra set of clothes and dressed in a hurry. "I'm taking this kid back to his mom. You coming?"

His jaw flexed and his gaze flowed over Alex, a testosterone tension filling the air. "I'll take my truck."

With that, we were on the move again, heading back to 'Bottoms Up,' me driving the SUV with the windows down to air out the smell of shit, and O'Shea following behind in his truck. But what would we do afterward? Would O'Shea come with me back to the farmhouse? Would he let me help him? Would he tell me he loved me back?

My gut twisted at the thought of losing him after we'd been through so much together. Because I knew better than anyone else that if O'Shea wasn't strong enough, this would be his last two weeks thinking like the man I knew before becoming just like Alex. If all I had with him were two weeks, then I wanted every precious moment I could get.

20

'Bottoms Up' was dark. Then again, it was like four in the morning, and even a strip bar shuts down at some point. I pulled over half a block away, eyeing up the building. I'd phoned Jewel and left her a message before we'd left O'Shea's house, telling her we were on our way.

Scrubbing my hands over my face, I waited a few moments before getting out of the SUV, the snow and wind curling around me, tangling my hair.

Alex slid out of the vehicle, sniffing the ground. "Wolf pack," he whispered, putting one claw to his lips.

Great, just what I needed. I waved once at O'Shea, and he got out of his truck, trudging through the snow in nothing but jeans, boots, and a t shirt.

"Aren't you cold?"

"No."

I squinted at him, blinking in surprise. As the snow hit his skin, little bursts of steam went upward. Shit, he was further along in the changes than I would have thought.

"You stay here, make sure no one else comes in after me," I said.

Frowning, O'Shea shook his head. "No. You aren't going in there alone."

"Listen." I put a hand on his chest, the heat radiating off him pulsing right through my gloves. "You are not in the best state of mind. I'm going in, and coming right back out."

"With the kid?"

"Yes, with the kid."

"You can't carry him and manage doors at the same time."

He glared at me, dark orbs floating with amber bits; my heart lurched. He was right, damn it.

"Fine. You carry the kid; I'll get the doors. Alex, you stick close."

The werewolf sat up on his haunches and gave me a sharp salute. "Yuppy doody!"

O'Shea picked up Ricky's body, slinging it over his shoulder with ease.

I led the way, one sword drawn just in case. The snow crunched under our feet, and was about the only sound I could hear. "Boys, you getting anything?"

Alex shook his head, and O'Shea glared at me. "I'm not a fucking scent hound."

I shrugged, for once not giving the sharp retort I normally would. He was going to be touchy for a while, getting used to using all his new found senses. Taking a slow, even breath, I put my hand on the front door, giving it a quick twist, expecting it to be locked. The door eased open, and a burly old man blinked up at us. "Heard you might be coming, leave the body here. I'll get it to Jewel."

"Fine," I said, pointing at the ground. "Put him down."

O'Shea laid Ricky on the doorstep and then grabbed my arm. "We need to leave. Right now."

I didn't question him, just turned and walked away as fast as I could without running. Our job was done, Ricky was delivered and now—

Three werewolves burst out of the building behind us, howling and snarling. Son of a bitch! This was what I'd wanted to avoid. O'Shea threw me behind him and I hit the snow, hard, sliding a good ten feet before tumbling to a stop.

Alex and O'Shea were back to back, the three werewolves surrounding them. Shit!

"Come on, you cocksuckers!" I got the attention of the smallest of the three. A thick gray pelt and bright green eyes peered at me, his muzzle pulling back in a wicked snarl before he leapt at me.

I yanked the whip from off my waist, snapping it through the air like a lion tamer, nailing the wolf in the face. He yelped, but kept coming, and I swirled the whip around again, getting it coiled around his neck. Like a giant leash, I yanked on it, putting all my weight into it. Around me, I could hear the howls and sounds of flesh being torn, but I couldn't look away to see how the boys were doing.

The gray wolf snarled at me then tried to bite through the whip, whimpering when his tongue and lips came in contact with it. A surprised look passed over his face, and I laughed.

"Woven with silver, asshole," I said, jerking it again, biting it deeper into the flesh around his neck. He growled and leapt at me. I dropped back, let him go over the top of me as I held up my sword. His momentum and the sharp blade did the trick. Rolling to the side, I missed most of the entrails sliding out of his body onto the white snow. He landed with a thud, crashing to the ground in utter stillness. A flick of my wrist and the whip uncoiled. Spinning, I turned to see things hadn't gone as badly as I thought.

The other two wolves were laid out, one with his neck obviously broken, head looking like it had been screwed on backwards, and the third was missing the front portion of his throat.

O'Shea stood in the middle of it, Alex cowering at his feet, tail thumping lightly in the snow.

"I have to go," he said, turning away from me.

"Liam, don't, this isn't as bad as you think it is." I called after him. He wasn't heading toward his truck, but in the opposite direction, toward the badlands and the open plains. Shit.

He said nothing else, just loped off into the darkness, his shadow fading until Alex and I were alone in the middle of the road, surrounded by bodies and blood.

The creature inside him raged. He should have killed all the wolves, including Alex. It had taken every last ounce of his strength to still his hands and teeth, to keep from tearing out the submissive wolf's throat. Then to walk away, turn his back and run, not only from Alex, but from Rylee. It tore a hole in him, the creature he was becoming not appreciative of the finer points of life.

Mates don't leave mates. Call to her, she will come. It was as if a voice that was not his own spoke, a new voice, one that had no problem killing, no problem with bloodshed. She'd said she loved him, but how could she now? What if he ended up like Alex, trapped in a body and a mind that wouldn't allow him anything but a submissive life?

He groaned into the icy wind, relishing the feel of it on his skin. It felt like there was a fire burning inside of him, scouring away what was left of the human he'd been, replacing it with the monster he was to become.

There was no way he'd be able to live a life now, not as he'd wanted, not even with Rylee. How could she be with him? It wasn't possible. The look in her eyes, the soft acceptance, the understanding and love; she couldn't know his thoughts, how he'd considered her fragile skin for biting into as much as for screwing.

Ducking his head, he ran into the wind, heading toward the badlands. He didn't know why, but the monster inside of him spurred him onward. It was better this way—his leaving—better for everyone.

Most of all, better for Rylee. And if it was the last thing he did, he would keep her safe, even if it was from himself.

Jewel called me three days after we left Ricky on her doorstep, sobbing, asking me to come to the kid's funeral. I declined. I also reversed the funds in my account; I couldn't take money for finding Ricky, not when I still felt like his death was, in part, my fault. It didn't matter that there were gunshot wounds, or that he'd been dead long before I found him, or had even started looking. My head and heart didn't always agree on what was my fault and what wasn't. This was just one of those cases that dredged up the fact I'd lost more kids than I'd saved. That simple fact was beginning to wear me down.

Two weeks came and went, the full moon crested and began to wane, and still there was no word from Liam. Thus far, I'd refused to Track him—if he wanted to deal with this alone, it was his choice. I was trying to respect that, but it was hard. By now, he was either just like Alex, stuck in a body caught between animal and human, or he was able to shift back and forth. With no word, and no sign of him, I feared the worst.

A phone call to Louisa had only intensified my fears.

"If Bear clawed him, it *could* have infected him with the shifting virus, but I doubt it. Most likely though, it was something else that got in the wound. Saliva is what carries it." I must have been silent too long as she went on with her explanation.

"There was no way you could have known what he was going through, Rylee. The changes are so subtle when a human becomes a shifter; even I didn't notice. Child, not even your second sight would have given you a clue to what was happening to him until he had already shifted."

There was a shuffle on the other end and, to my surprise, Doran came on.

"Hello, beautiful Tracker. I hear your man has gone missing. My deepest condolences."

I grit my teeth. "Yeah, thanks."

"I wanted to tell you that you made it much safer here by taking out Jensen. Truly. For that, I will give you a favor. Free of charge."

As much as he'd helped me, I was suspicious. "Why would you do that?"

His words rang alarm bells, as if he'd come at me with his teeth prepped for bleeding me dry. "I want you to trust me; I want you to let me help you."

I hung up the phone, shaking. His words were an echo of Faris's, and I didn't want any reminder of the vampire.

Thanks to all that was holy, *he* hadn't made a repeat appearance, though I dreamed of Berget several times. Normal dreams, reminders of the past, and nothing more. I wasn't sure if I was happy about that or not.

Mulling over Louisa's words, I rehashed the scene in her home in my mind, slowly realizing the mistake we'd made. I'd made. Liam had had open wounds and Alex had lain across them, drooling and bloodied around the mouth.

Alex had, because of my ineptitude, been the one to turn Liam. I slumped down against the kitchen counters, tucking my head between my knees, arms over my head. Shit, again, the blame for the loss of someone close to me lay squarely on my shoulders. With my face covered, I let the tears slip out, one by one, dripping onto the floor.

Worse, I'd made the mistake of telling Milly that O'Shea had contracted either bear- or wolf-shifting virus, and since then she hadn't eased her campaign to make me 'see the light.'

As if thinking about her had rung a summons bell, her footsteps eased into the kitchen.

"Let me guess," Milly said, coming closer. "You found out your agent man contracted the werewolf virus from Alex."

I still hadn't figured out what was going on with her, why she'd changed so drastically, what had happened? When I brought it up, she blew me off, said I was imagining things. Which only made me realize that there was indeed something wrong.

I lifted my head, wondering what had happened to the girl I'd known, the one I'd have called sister if someone asked. She wasn't the Milly I'd grown up with—that girl was gone. Now she was almost a stranger, someone I couldn't predict and no longer understood. There were no words in me to answer her, the guilt and blame lay truthfully on my shoulders. Having her rub it in did not help. It only made me angry. It was bad enough to lose O'Shea, but to know she was slipping away from me too only intensified my emotions and made me lash out.

"Go fuck one of your men," I said, lowering my head again.

She crouched beside me, the swoosh of her skirt and the scent of rose petals washing over me. I had to give her credit, she always did smell good.

"So I was right, whatever. Get rid of him. You can't keep Alex, not as long as Giselle and I are here. When you were alone it was no big deal. Now, you can see what I was worried about. And don't worry about the agent man, you'll find somebody else; I always do."

I wanted to shove her away from me, scream at her that she was wrong. Alex was my responsibility. But logically I knew she was right; I was the only one immune from his bite, or even his saliva, god damn it! She was wrong about Liam, though. No one could replace him. There was too much history, too much between us to wash it away.

Alex was as much my family now as she and Giselle. I couldn't choose between them.

"I can't," I said.

"Rylee, please, I'm not trying to be a bitch. I just don't want to turn into a werewolf like O'Shea. And I don't want that for Giselle either. Can you imagine a werewolf that was pretty much insane? You'd have to kill her," she said, tucking her head beside mine, slipping an arm around me.

I pushed her arm off and stood up. She was right. Grabbing my leather jacket, I stepped outside into the cold, snow falling heavily in the late afternoon sun. Alex blitzed about like a madman, chasing imaginary prey. What the hell was I going to do?

The barn was empty now with Eve training in New Mexico; that at least was one concern gone for the moment. Even with the Harpy nowhere near, Milly hadn't let up her tirade from the moment I'd gotten back. My heart was torn, and I stood there for a long time, staring at nothing, wracking my brain. There was the creak of the back door being opened, and then a frail set of arms wound around my waist. Giselle put herself under my one arm and I gave her a half hug.

"Why do you cry, Rylee?"

I thought for a minute, trying to put it all into one nutshell.

"Because life isn't fair."

She snorted. "Ah, well, that's true. But I never said it would be. I said you should follow your heart, didn't I?"

Giving me a quick squeeze, she left me standing on the back porch, watching Alex romp and play by himself in the snow. Leaping up, he'd bite at the falling flakes, then diving forward, he'd bury himself until only his tail showed. Milly was the sister of my heart, the person I thought I could trust with anything, the one who'd been my friend for years. Alex was, in essence, a child that would die on his own, but also a loyal friend willing to put his life on the line for me. Could I let him go, knowing I was sentencing him to death? I wrapped my arms around myself. Life was changing. I was changing, and it hurt me to think I would be walking away from someone I thought of as family.

For a brief second, I gave in and Tracked O'Shea, needing to feel him close even if it was just his emotions. Rage flooded me, bloodlust and shame following close on its heels. I sucked in a sharp breath, biting back tears and shutting down the connection between us. *Please God let him be able to shift form, please don't let him be trapped as Alex was.*

I stood there a few minutes longer, my mind whirling with possibilities, decisions and outcomes. None of which I liked. There was really only one way to do this, no matter how much I hated to.

Stepping back into the kitchen, I looked over at my friend. Milly sat at the table, her hands folded on top, an air of tension thrumming between us.

"Have you made a decision," she asked, green eyes wide with hope.

"Yes," I replied, and she smiled, relief on her face.

"I knew you'd do the right thing, Rylee."

I didn't smile back at her; this was the only way I could see working for everyone. Taking a long slow breath in, I held it until I was dizzy. Letting the air out, I said the words, knowing they would change everything.

"Alex stays." I gripped the edge of the table. "And you have to move out."

COMING JANUARY 2017 FROM TALOS PRESS

RAISING INNOCENCE

A Rylee Adamson Novel
Book 3

"My name is Rylee, and I am a Tracker."

When children go missing, and the Humans have no leads, I'm the one they call. I am their last hope in bringing home the lost ones. I salvage what they cannot.

The FBI wants me on their team. Bad enough that they are dangling bait they know I can't resist.

The catch? It's on the other side of the ocean.

And if I want what they're offering, I have to help them with a salvage gone terribly, terribly wrong.

But this time, I have no back up. I have no Plan B.

And I have no O'Shea.

$7.99 mass market paperback
978-1-940456-97-3

AN EXCERPT FROM RAISING INNOCENCE

Tracking Milly was easy, something I did without even thinking, really. She was the first person I'd ever Tracked on purpose, the first person whose life threads had hummed inside my skull, a vibration all their own.

I followed her threads through Bismarck to the northeast side of town. There wasn't much here, at least nothing that should have drawn her. She'd always loved the glitz and glamor of the city life.

"Stop thinking about her as your friend, Rylee."

A long slow breath in helped to calm me, then I let it out and, with it, let go of Milly once and for all.

Milly's threads drew me to a beautiful office building, newer, but with architectural touches that showed a modern design with a nod to the past. Squinting my eyes and using my second sight, I could just see the faint outlines of what had to be the Coven's symbol, a full moon with the faint image of a wolf inside it, on the front door. What the hell, why not storm the Coven's main building? One last hurrah for Giselle and me. The witch was inside, resting, by the feel of things. Not sleeping, but relaxing. I had no way of knowing how many other Coven members there were.

"Maybe you should wait here," I said, thinking about how to get to the top of the three-story building and past any number of Coven members with Giselle, who was frail on a good day.

"I can bloody well walk. I'm not dead yet," she snapped at me.

Oh, there was one of those bad traits she mentioned. A smile flitted across my lips, but disappeared as I stepped out of the Jeep.

The ever-blowing wind of North Dakota seared my eyeballs, making them tear up. Damn it all.

Blindly, I groped in the back seat, grabbed the two bottles of salt water, and then shut the door with my hip. I wasn't worried about being heard or detected. I was an Immune, unable to be detected or affected directly with magic; it was a perk that went with the territory.

"Do you have a plan?" Giselle asked.

"The usual."

"So you mean no plan."

"Exactly."

Plans went awry, and people fell apart. In my mind, it was better to always go in hot, and adjust yourself as the shit hit the fan.

We walked to the front door and I hesitated. I might not set off any alarm system, but Giselle would. I glanced over at her and she lifted a single eyebrow at me. We'd done this many times before she'd lost her sanity and we needed very few actual words to communicate. I handed her the two bottles of salt water first.

Then I crouched down so I could carry her on my back. My crossed sword sheath dug into me, but it was a minor irritant. Did my Immunity flow over Giselle like a cloak?

Fucked if I know, but it was the best we could do with what we had.

Giselle's ability lay in reading people, seeing the future, seeing the past. But she had once been a wicked ass fighter. She'd learned to fight because, like me, her abilities didn't provide the sort of power that someone like Milly had. We were both fighters in the physical sense, and could kick Milly's ass around town in that arena; our one major advantage over her. Of course, the chances were good that the bitch witch wasn't alone. Nor did it help that Giselle was so out of shape, and wasted from the madness.

The doorknob was cool under my touch and I twisted it with care, easing the door open. Poking my head in, I spotted stairs across the lobby, and no one waiting for us.

Yet.

Shifting Giselle on my back, I walked as fast as I could across the lobby, doing my best to soften the sound of my boots on the marble floor.

"Opulent for a Coven who has no ties to the world, isn't it?" Giselle noted, her voice low.

I was thinking along the same lines. Milly had claimed the Coven had no ties with the secular world, that they were woefully ignorant of the humans, and even at times, other supernaturals. But this place didn't give me that feeling, not by a long shot.

There was even a computer at the desk, which meant that there were humans here.

We made it all the way to the third floor before I put Giselle down and pulled my two blades out of their sheaths. There was only a single door between us and Milly, and my heart pounded. I could do this; I had to.

My hands were slick with sweat, my muscles trembled, and it wasn't the climb of the stairs that was doing it.

Giselle reached over and put a hand on my forearm. "Steady, Rylee. This must be done. Much as we hate it."

A sharp nod was all I managed. One breath in, I lifted my right leg and slammed the heel of my boot into the door, banging it open.

Milly wore the same skintight green dress she'd had on the previous day, and had her back to us. Four other people in the room faced us, hands raised. Shit, four witches against the two of us. The odds were definitely not in our favor.

The witches facing us wove spells, and based on the cannonballs rapidly headed in my direction, they knew to choose spells that wouldn't directly attack me, instead opting to hurt me with other things. Big nasty things that would smash my brains in if I wasn't careful. Shit, shit, shit! Milly had told them.

"They know!" Was all I managed before spinning to dodge the cannonball that came spinning toward my head.

Giselle threw the two bottles of salt water, one right after the other, but only doused a single witch. Not enough.

Milly had set the trap, and we'd walked right into it.

"Giselle, get out of here!" I yelled, knowing that she wouldn't leave, but I had to try.

Milly moved away from me as I dodged and ducked the cantaloupe-sized iron balls. It looked like they were throwing two or three each, six balls zinging around the room at a speed I could only just keep ahead of. I tried to keep track of Milly while I dodged the balls, but it was impossible to do both. Dodging the balls became my main focus.

I hit the ground, rolling toward the closest witch, a man who stood about my height with short blond hair. That was all I registered before I grabbed his ankle and jerked him off his feet. He hit the ground with a grunt, two cannonballs dropping with him, and I moved on to the next witch. If I could disrupt their spells enough, we had a chance.

Not a good chance, but a chance nonetheless.

"Rylee, left," Giselle yelled.

I jerked my body to the left, three cannonballs slicing through the air where I'd been. I flipped up to my feet and ran at the one closest to me, my right sword slicing through the air, taking off her arm at the elbow. She screamed, her face a blur to me as I spun.

One of the cannonballs caught me, slamming into my lower back with a force that knocked the wind out of me and sent me sailing across the room. I hit the far wall, stars dancing in front of my eyes as the pain in my back spread. My fingers and toes tingled, and I could move them, but not fast enough.

The cannonballs caught me then. As they hit me the spells diffused, but that wasn't enough to stop the impacts, although apparently it was enough to let the witch turn her attention to the cannonballs her fellows had dropped.

Bones crunched. I felt them snap and twist. I slumped, unable to dodge what was coming at me. Pain flared but disappeared as the next ball hit me, leaving a new impression. Fast and hard, I couldn't see them pinned face-first against the wall, but I sure as shit on a Troll could feel them.

I was so fucked.

"Enough!" Giselle's voice rose above the sound of my body being shattered, the grunts of air as they escaped me. I could do nothing to stop the slide of my body down the wall, barely catching myself with my left arm. The right was shattered at the elbow; I barely remembered it happening. What shocked me was the fact that they stopped at Giselle's command, and then the pain rolled over me, and for a moment I blacked out.

As I came to, voices floated around me.

"You have been misled. As have we. I see that she even left a stunt double."

Daughter of a whore, did that mean that Milly wasn't here? A part of me was glad, and the other part was just fucking pissed.

"She said you'd claim that."

"Convenient," Giselle said, her voice dry. There was the rustle of someone's clothes, then, "The least you could do is ease her pain since you attacked us first. You do have the proper herbs, don't you?"

There was a sputter of disbelief, and then a pair of hands went around my neck. I opened my eyes to look up into the face of a freaking angel. She was stunning, the lines of her face reminiscent of the classic beauties, feminine and soft, full lips, huge blue-green eyes framed with dark lashes and a button nose.

Her voice was high-pitched, yet easy on the ears. "Milly told us you could hold back your Immunity on your hands? Do it and I will heal you."

Giselle came into my line of sight and gave me a nod. She thought it was a good idea, though I wasn't so sure. With an effort, I peeled my Immunity back, my fingers bared to whatever magic the witch would use on me.

Her fingers touched mine. "Hold still, this will hurt, but it will be quick and your body will be whole."

A soft tingle was the first of it, and then my broken bones did a jig, yanking back into place. I bit my tongue on the scream that rose up, shaking as my body reknit itself. I was shocked—and not just at the pain.

Milly had always claimed that healing like this wasn't possible. That it wasn't *just* not one of her talents, but that you couldn't heal people with magic.

Fool me once, shame on you. Fool me twice, shame on me. Fool me a third time, and I'm going to run you the fuck through.

Panting, I lay still while my body finished mending itself under the guidance of the witch's magic. The pain slowly lessened and the click of bone snapping back together slowed until there was nothing but the beat of my heart in my ears.

I pushed myself into a sitting position, my back against the wall, one sword across my lap the other on the floor beside me.

"Cannonballs. Nasty, but effective," I said, pushing one of the iron balls with my left foot.

The man I'd stabbed sat up from across the room, the healer stepping away from him. The woman whose arm I'd removed was not in the room. How long had I been out for? "We thought it pertinent, considering your innate ability to avoid magic, to be prepared for an attack."

A snort escaped me. "Attack? I'm not here for you. I'm here for Milly."

The witches stilled around us. Apparently, honesty is not always the best policy.

Giselle stepped between us, as if her frail body could withstand even one blow from a cannonball. "Milly has betrayed not only us, but your Coven as well."

The woman, the one who'd healed me, held her hand up for silence. "The rest of you may stay, but I will lead this. I knew Milly the best. She was like my sister."

My stomach felt as if it had been yanked out and dropped from the window, the words striking me as easily as one of those gods-be-damned cannonballs. This woman was like Milly's sister? Then what the hell was I? And why did I care?

I was a goddamned fucking idiot. That was what I was.

ABOUT THE AUTHOR

Shannon Mayer is the *USA Today* bestselling author of the Rylee Adamson novels, the Elemental series, and numerous paranormal romance, urban fantasy, mystery, and suspense novels. She lives in the southwestern tip of Canada with her husband, son, and numerous other animals.